I ordered a cappuccino. Danny Celestino introduced the two women—Ann Walters and Libby Trask—as his coworkers at Village Cat People. "You know, Miss Nestleton, we've heard about your work."

I smiled. "Well, when you've been in the theater as long as I have, sooner or later a few people hear of you . . . happily."

Libby Trask fairly hissed in response. "We're not talking about the theater. We're talking about your other activities. Crime."

"We need your help," Danny said pleadingly. "Martha Lorenz was not killed by any street criminal. She was assassinated. It was a cold-blooded, premeditated murder made to look like a mugging that got out of hand."

"Those are some very strong assertions," I said. "Do you have any proof to back them up?"

Danny said, his passion rising, "A week before it happened Martha told us she was marked for death. She said she was being hunted. We asked her who would want to kill her. She wouldn't tell us." He added, "All she said was a single word."

"And the word was . . . ?"

"*Aspettando.*"

A
CAT ON THE
CUTTING EDGE

An Alice Nestleton Mystery

Lydia Adamson

A SIGNET BOOK

SIGNET
Published by the Penguin Group
Penguin Books USA Inc., 375 Hudson Street,
New York, New York 10014, U.S.A.
Penguin Books Ltd, 27 Wrights Lane,
London W8 5TZ, England
Penguin Books Australia Ltd, Ringwood,
Victoria, Australia
Penguin Books Canada Ltd, 10 Alcorn Avenue,
Toronto, Ontario, Canada M4V 3B2
Penguin Books (N.Z.) Ltd, 182–190 Wairau Road,
Auckland 10, New Zealand

Penguin Books Ltd, Registered Offices:
Harmondsworth, Middlesex, England

First published by Signet, an imprint of Dutton Signet,
a division of Penguin Books USA Inc.

First Printing, October, 1994
10 9 8 7 6 5 4 3 2 1

The first chapter of this book previously appeared in *A Cat With No Regrets*, the eighth volume in this series.

Ⓢ REGISTERED TRADEMARK—MARCA REGISTRADA

Printed in the United States of America

PUBLISHER'S NOTE:
This is a work of fiction. Names, characters, places, and incidents either are the product of the author's imagination or are used fictitiously, and any resemblance to actual persons, living or dead, events, or locales is entirely coincidental.

A
CAT ON THE
CUTTING EDGE

1

I never had any problem cutting my Maine coon cat's claws. Following the advice of another cat lover I knew, I would merely sneak up on Bushy when he was sleeping and clip one nail before he knew what was happening. For every snooze he took, he lost a sharp claw. At the end of the afternoon—*voila!* he had a manicure.

But Pancho, my lunatic half-tailed refugee from the ASPCA, was another matter. He never slept. At least he never slept while I was awake. So, a few times a year, I had to dump him into the carrier and take him to the vet to perform the honors.

Now Pancho, even though he spent his entire day fleeing from imaginary enemies, was always very easy to get into his carrier and no problem at all once inside of it. In fact, he seemed to enjoy the whole process— that is, until we arrived at the vet's office and he saw the dreaded clippers in the doctor's hand.

The only thing I had to do was to bribe him with a little saffron rice, fed to him just before I dumped him into the box. For some reason beyond human comprehension, Pancho loved saffron rice with a passion.

So, that's what I did on that Tuesday afternoon in April. I gave him a small bowl of saffron rice and waited until he had annihilated the offering, smacking his lips. Then I opened his battered old carrier, a top loader, and picked him up.

To put it mildly, all hell broke loose. Pancho went ballistic. First he tensed. Then, as I started to push him into the box, he began to struggle. I held on tighter, he struggled more. I warned him, tapping him on the nose. Then he became a wildcat and I just couldn't hold him.

"What is the matter with you?" I demanded. "You always liked your carrier." He sat down about ten feet away from me and eyed me balefully. I approached him slowly. He didn't run.

But the moment I picked him up he started to fight again. And I lost my temper and I fought back and he started to screech and I started to yell and then I felt a sharp stab of pain on my forearm and I dropped him.

Pancho had bloodied me! I couldn't believe it. I sat down on a chair and almost wept.

"How could you do that, Pancho?" I implored. He looked totally unconcerned. I searched for Bushy, for spiritual help, but my Maine coon had vanished.

It was a very bad time for this to happen. Things had definitely not been going my way as of late. My niece, Alison Chevigny, with whom I had been brought together so wonderfully and unexpectedly in France during my unsuccessful fling at cinematic stardom, was head over heels in love. And after having stayed with me for six months, she had decided to go off and live with the man. She was moving out and I knew I would miss her.

In addition, the featured role I had been promised in an upcoming Broadway sleuther had evaporated when the producer met me and realized I was the same actress he'd wrestled with—and lost—ten years ago.

In addition, one of my very best cat-sitting clients, Mrs. Ridout, was moving to Charlotte, North Carolina, with her husband, Jock, and their cat, Reggie.

In addition, the part I had been offered in the production of a TV movie about the prison life of the woman who murdered the famous Scarsdale Diet Doctor was written out of the script at the last moment. I had really been counting on that money. Was there any other sane reason to have accepted the role in the first place?

And, to make matters even worse, my special friend, Tony Basillio, had been acting very strangely lately, accusing me of infidelity and various other crimes.

Oh yes, it was a bad time for me . . . a bad time for Pancho to have become so aggressive . . . a very bad time indeed.

I tried to reason with the gray cat who was now half hidden under one end of the sofa, ready to make a run for the hallway if I approached.

"Pancho, I want you to listen to me now. Sooner or later you're going to have to get your nails clipped. And for that to happen I have to get you to the vet. And to do that I have to put you in your box, Pancho. It's a routine we've followed many times—right? . . . Isn't that right, Pancho? So why this sudden antagonism toward that carrier? What is going on with you, you old fiend?"

But he would not be swayed by reason. I realized that the only way I'd get him into the box was to knock him unconscious. And I was not prepared to do that.

I glared at him. He slouched lower and glared back. We were obviously experiencing one of those very rare and very malevolent failures to communicate.

Wearily, I went to the phone and dialed Dr. Leon, my new vet, who had come recommended by John Cerise, an old friend and the most knowledgeable cat man I know. Leon's practice was down in the Village—not my neighborhood but only ten minutes away by cab. Peg Oates, his assistant, took my call. When she heard I wanted to cancel the appointment, she switched me to Dr. Leon.

"Dr. Leon, it's Alice Nestleton. I'm sorry to mess up your schedule this afternoon, but I can't get my cat into his carrier."

"Don't worry," he said in his kindly voice. "We'll reschedule when kitty is up to it."

I liked Dr. Leon. I had seen him only three times, twice with Bushy and once with Pancho, and each time he had impressed me more, particularly when we thought that Bushy had a serious pancreatic deficiency. He told Bushy and me exactly what he was going to do each step of the way and why he was doing it.

"I'm searching for the by-product enzyme trypsin," he had said as he ordered the tests. "If it's not there, then it has to be put there, or Bushy will not be able to digest and absorb food properly."

Leon was a short, powerfully built man in his late thirites and he just seemed to scoop his patients up preparatory to working his healing magic.

Just as I was about to hang up, Dr. Leon asked, "Did you ever hear of the Village Cat People?"

I couldn't help laughing at the name. It sounded like the cult following for a bad Hollywood movie. Or the title of the movie itself. Then I got myself under control.

"Sorry," I said, "it's just that the name is so funny. No, Dr. Leon, I've never heard of the Village Cat People. Who are they?"

"A group of veterinary technicians who make house calls. A sort of feline EMS. Full service. They're not vets, but close enough for what they do."

"House calls?"

"Sure. They'll come to your home and tranquilize your cat. Or corral him and transport him. Or do anything, short of actual veterinary diagnosis and treatment."

"How ingenious," I said. What a shame I hadn't known about the Village Cat People before.

Dr. Leon gave me their phone number. I wrote it down and then asked, "Are they expensive?"

"Very reasonable."

"Then please let the appointment stand, Dr. Leon. Only make it an hour or so later. I'll call the Village Cat People and have them come here and give Pancho something to get him in hand. Then I'll bring him over."

"They can also clip his nails," Dr. Leon said.

For a moment I was put out. Didn't he want to do the clipping? I always considered that a kind of honor. "Well, I'd prefer you do it. Pancho already knows you."

"Okay. Fine. I'll be expecting you," he confirmed.

I hung up and called the Village Cat People. The pleasant-sounding woman at the other end of the line took down all the necessary information on me and the reluctant patient, Pancho. It was all handled professionally, not at all the way an outfit with a kind of whimsical, post-hippie name like Village Cat People might have dealt with the situation. The VCP representative quoted a price for the visit and the tranquilizing injection. I agreed. She told me that one of her associates—Martha Lorenz—would arrive at my apartment within the hour.

I was greatly relieved, almost giddy. Imagine. A professional Pancho mover would be here shortly.

Then Alison came in, wondering why I was looking so disarranged. I explained what had happened. She didn't seem truly interested in my little cat problem, though. But I suppose that's the way it is when you're in love; nothing else really counts. And Alison was definitely in love. Hugely. Almost like a schoolgirl. But Alison was no schoolgirl. She was twenty-four, a grown woman who'd been married and widowed during her time in France. And now she had found love again. I knew she had it bad when she cut off all her beautiful golden hair. Only a woman in love cuts her hair that radically.

"Any calls?" she asked sweetly, going into the kitchen to put the kettle on. Alison drank a great deal of coffee. As did I. But she'd brought in her own fancy coffeepot months ago, chastising me heavily for my instant coffee fetish.

Any calls? That meant, of course, Had *he* called? *He* being one Felix Drinnan, a fifty-one-year-old psychiatrist who had more money than God, both from his practice and his family, and who seemed to be as in love with Alison as she was with him. He owned and lived in an entire four-story house in the West Village, on Barrow Street. I didn't dislike him, but I couldn't say I liked him, either. And I found it strange that Alison would fall in love with a man old enough to be her father, someone who collected ancient coins and antique quilts. After all, her late husband, Hugh Chevigny, had been much closer to her own age, and he had been a gifted cat trainer. Well, it was stupid to make comparisons, but the whole thing confused me and made me unhappy.

I poked my head into the small kitchen. "Felix didn't call," I said, "but to be honest I was so upset about what was happening with Pancho that the phone might have rung without my even hearing it."

"Understandable, Aunt Alice," she said, sweetly again. Alison was becoming positively niecish—if any such word exists.

Then she asked, "What time are those people coming over?"

"What people?"

"The ones you just told me about. The cat people."

"Oh, no, that's their collective name. Only one person is coming. I think her name is Marjorie Lorenz . . . no, Martha Lorenz."

"Shall I stay and help you?"

"How are you going to help?" I retorted, a bit caustically, as if in all the time she had been with me she had not helped me at all. Which was untrue. She had helped me in every way possible.

"Well, Aunt Alice, if Pancho is determined not to be caught, it might take more than you *and* the cat person to catch him and give him that shot."

"Really, Alison, you needn't worry. Miss Lorenz does things like this for a living. We'll be okay."

She poured coffee into each of two mugs on the counter. She was making a cup for me without even asking. For some reason that irritated me. It seemed condescending. She mixed it properly, a little less than half a cup for me, then a third of a Sweet'n Low packet. Tony Basillio had once told me that I drink coffee like his uncle from the old country. Now, that I took as a compliment.

Alison handed me my coffee. We stayed there together in the kitchen while we drank. She held her cup as if she were warming her palms, as if it were wintertime and there was no heat in the apartment.

"You know," she mused, "I really thought I

would never be in love again. I mean, after
Hugh killed himself, the idea of having anything to do with another man seemed so remote . . . absurd . . . impossible. And now
here I am . . . thousands of miles away from
Hugh . . . from his grave . . . all those memories . . . and all I can think of is Felix.
Hugh seems like some sort of . . ." She
didn't finish the sentence.

Had she wanted to involve me in a discussion of one's responsibility to the dead? Of
what constitutes loyalty to their memory? I
didn't know what she was talking about, really. Maybe she was just talking. Maybe she
was a bit frightened about making the
move.

". . . though sometimes I do call Felix,
Hugh," she said, sounding a little bitter.

"It's a common thing," I said soothingly.

"Not when you're making love."

I was saved from further discussion by
the low throb of the street door buzzer. "The
cat people are upon us," Alison said in a
conspiratorial whisper.

I buzzed the cat person in and then
stepped outside the apartment into the hallway to await her ascent. It was standard
procedure for people in my building, because one could easily identify the climber
by leaning out over the railing and looking
down at the landings below. If it was one of
the criminal element, one just ran back into
the apartment and called 911. It wasn't that

the neighborhood was crime-ridden; it wasn't. The problem was Bellevue, the massive city hospital, and its enormous network of outpatient clinics that support alcoholics, drug addicts, released mental patients, and so many other unfortunates. These people tended to wander, and show up in strange hallways.

"She's still ringing," I heard Alison call from inside the apartment.

"Please buzz her in again. The door's probably stuck. It happens from time to time."

Alison buzzed for a long time, but the bell in the apartment kept ringing and I saw no one climbing the stairs. It must be that wretched door again. And if it was stuck, it had to be opened from the inside.

"I'll go down," I told Alison.

As I descended, I silently, and then not so silently cursed Pancho as the cause of all this nonsense. It was the last time that cat would ever see any saffron rice in his little yellow bowl. I felt positively vengeful.

When I reached the bottom landing I could see the woman's figure behind the clouded glass of the door. Yes, it was obviously stuck. She was still ringing and Alison was still buzzing back. It was like a bumblebee concerto with two psychotic conductors. I just hoped I could get the door open and put an end to all the racket.

I did manage to open it. What a beautiful

young woman, I thought as I looked into Martha Lorenz's very pale eyes. Perhaps Pancho will be smitten.

But she did not step inside.

I smiled reassuringly at her. Then she pitched forward, her hands brushing against my body as she fell to the floor. I did not scream until I saw that her throat had been slit.

2

Three days later I was doing exactly the same thing at the same time in the same place—waiting for a representative of the Village Cat People to arrive and sedate Pancho enough to transport him to the vet.

But, of course, the interior of the event had been changed . . . all changed. I waited tight lipped and white knuckled. I could not shake that murdered woman from my consciousness. It was the first time I had ever seen a slit throat. It was the first time a body wet with blood had fallen onto me.

Tony Basillio was playing with Bushy near the window. He had come over to lend me moral support. My niece had to make some last-minute moving arrangements and had left the apartment early in the morning. Tony was wearing a faded denim shirt hanging loose over paint-smeared jeans and the remnants of running shoes. It was easy to tell that he was a stage designer of sorts, but it wasn't easy to tell that he was past forty. Wasn't it odd? The longer we remained lovers, the younger he seemed to become. Oh, but not I.

"Where's the criminal element?" he called out. "Bushy's whipping my ass at checkers. But maybe I could take old Pancho in a game of ticktacktoe."

"I haven't the slightest idea," I said. "Let the Cat People find him and cart him off."

"You're really down on poor old Pancho, aren't you?" Tony moved close to me and ran his hand affectionately along the side of my neck.

"I'm down on Pancho. I'm down on myself. Face facts, Tony. It was my incompetence and Pancho's lunacy that got that young woman killed."

"You can't be serious."

"Of course I am."

"You're talking stupid, Swede. Real stupid. There's no causality here at all. A creepy bastard followed her into the lobby. He put a knife at her throat. She refused to give up her bag. He slit her throat and emptied the purse and took the bag she was carrying with the items she carried around for cats— tranquilizers and that kind of stuff. She could have been accosted in any building, any time. The detective told us that three-quarters of the robberies in this precinct

happen that way—and half the killings.
Someone follows you into the building."

The buzzer rang just then. I absolutely
froze. I couldn't answer the doorbell in my
own apartment. I had that much terror and
loathing left over from the day of the murder.

Tony realized what was happening. He
pressed the button and then opened the
apartment door and stepped out into the
hall to await the climber. I closed my eyes
and folded my hands. What if the downstairs buzzer rang again? That would mean
the lobby door was stuck again. And it
would mean I'd have to go down there. And
perhaps there would be another corpse
falling through the doorway and into my
arms—in an almost loving embrace.

But the bell did not go off a second time,
and moments later Tony was ushering an
earnest young man into the apartment.

Earnest is not the word, really. Rather,
confident. Moving like a lemur in his low,
buckled boots, Danny Celestino, of the Village Cat People Inc., exuded confidence. He
was wearing tan work pants and a flak vest
over a dark T-shirt whose sleeves were
rolled up to highlight his perfectly muscled
arms. He was arrestingly handsome. One of
those remarkable New York faces with that
haunting synthesis of the blunt and the
beautiful . . . half angel, half thug. In fact, if
John Barrymore and John Garfield could

have had a son together, he'd look like Danny Celestino.

Protruding from one of the pockets of the Village Cat Person's vest were two serious-looking Syrettes.

He introduced himself formally. He made no mention of the tragedy. In fact, he said nothing at all about Martha Lorenz. He just set to work, reaching into his small bag and pulling out a pair of long, heavily padded gloves.

As I watched him draw on the gloves, slowly, carefully, it occurred to me that he was putting on a performance of sorts. *Oh, of course!* thought I, Danny Celestino is probably an out-of-work actor—as Martha Lorenz may have been—and perhaps everybody at the Village Cat People. I don't know why the realization seemed ludicrous, but it did. After all, half the service businesses in New York depend on the labor of out-of-work actors. So why not the Cat People?

"Here's the way it works," Celesino said. He had the slightest trace of a Brooklyn accent, as if he had kept it there through all the acting classes because he didn't want people to forget where he came from. As if anybody gave a damn.

With a tug on the Velcro flap of his vest pocket, he pulled out a Syrette, inspected it for a moment, and then slipped it back. "We use a safe and fast-acting tranquilizer.

It's best to inject at the base of the thigh, along the inside. Quick. No pain. The little darling konks—well, not completely. He just becomes so placid he thinks he's a roach." The young man obviously had a bizarre sense of humor, or perhaps he, too, was in shock still from Martha Lorenz's death.

After all, it might have been him three days prior at my door. Knocking, knocking at my door.

"It will go much easier," he said, smiling, "if I can count on your help."

I gave him an angry look, so fierce that he seemed to wince. No, there would be no help from this actress—this out-of-work actress. Not now. Learn the lines yourself. Sedate the cat yourself. I couldn't even move.

Tony stepped in. "I'll help you out," he said gallantly. Then he looked at me inquiringly. "In the kitchen or the bedroom, Swede?"

"I don't know. One or the other. If he's in the kitchen, he'll be up on the cabinet. If he's in the bedroom, probably hovering around the bookcase."

"He moves fast," Tony explained to the visitor.

"So do I," Danny retorted. They disappeared down the hallway.

I sat there listening to the frantic clamor. They thought they had cornered Pancho in the small kitchen, but he eluded them and headed for the bedroom. There he would make his last stand. I heard the scuffling and Tony's curses and Danny Celestino's very calm instructions to his new assistant. And then all was quiet.

Danny walked back into the living room first. Then Tony, carrying a supine and goofily peaceful Pancho. Into the carrier went the wild cat. Snap went the lid.

I wrote a check to the Village Cat People and the young man drove us to Dr. Leon's place. It was a nice gesture. He was probably off to an audition somewhere.

As for that nail-cutting visit to Dr. Leon— what can be said? The causal chain of guilt had touched the vet as well; he, too, had played an unwitting part in Martha Lorenz's murder. No matter that Tony called it nonsense. For it was Leon who had recommended the Village Cat People to me. He had set the karmic thing in motion and I had run with it until poor Martha lay dead in my lobby.

We said nothing about the murder— nothing. We each knew what the other was feeling and there was no way to dilute it. So Dr. Leon played the detached professional and I was the concerned cat owner and Pancho . . . Pancho was a blissed-out beatific.

The three of us—Tony, Pancho, and I— took a cab back to my apartment. Tony wanted to come up. He wanted to stay the night. My niece wouldn't mind, he coaxed.

"She never minds if you stay over," I explained to him. "The problem is that this is Alison's last night with me, so I think I should spend it just with her. You understand, don't you, Tony?"

"Okay, I guess I do. Do you want me to take Pancho up for you?"

"I can handle him," I said gently. With Tony, one had to be extremely careful when declining an offer of help. He was quite paranoid and would attribute the refusal to all kinds of bizarre motives.

He stayed in the cab. Pancho and I got out. It was a long climb up the stairs and I apologized to my beast for the many names I had called him over the past three days. He seemed unconcerned.

The moment we entered the apartment I released Pancho from his carrier. What he wanted to do was zoom off to continue his struggle with unseen enemies. But the flesh was not willing. He was still a tad disoriented. He wobbled out of the room. Bushy watched the proceedings wryly from his place on the sofa.

"Alison!" I called out. "I'm home."

There was no response.

Then I noticed that the three pieces of luggage that had been left where the living room and the hallway converge were gone.

For a moment I surmised theft. My heart

skipped a beat. But then I spotted the note on the coffee table, propped up against a book.

> DEAR AUNT ALICE,
> DECIDED TO GET STARTED EARLY. I HATE FAREWELLS, YOU KNOW, BUT THIS REALLY ISN'T FAREWELL—BECAUSE, AFTER ALL, I'M ONLY 20 BLOCKS OR SO DOWNTOWN. FELIX AND I EXPECT YOU FOR BRUNCH ON SUNDAY AT HIS BARROW STREET PLACE. 12 NOON. AND THANK YOU FOR EVERYTHING!
> —A

I sat down. Dejected. Hurt. When Alison told me she would be moving out, I began planning for this evening. I had secreted all kinds of little surprise gifts for her in the apartment—a new coffee mug, champagne, the works. I was going to make her a party to show her how great it had been to have her here and that I wished her all the happiness in the world with Felix. I had planned on it, looked forward to it. It never dawned on me that it wouldn't happen, that she would just be . . . *gone* . . . when I arrived home and that would be that.

Yes, yes, yes. The brunch was sure to be lovely. Sunday brunch at Felix's charming old brownstone on charming lil' old Barrow Street. Of course I would go; I'd never dream of turning down the invitation. But to hell with the stupid brunch. Oh, Alison!

I felt very alone. Bushy brushed against my leg and arched his back. I whisked him into my arms. He always seemed to understand—even when nobody else in the world did.

3

I arrived in front of Felix Drinnan's Barrow Street town house five minutes early. I was buzzed in promptly. Alison and Felix were dressed in the same shades of brown. They stood casually in the hall. I peeked into the massive dining room with its elegant oval cherrywood table.

"I see the table's not set. Are we eating in the kitchen?" I quipped.

Felix threw back his head and laughed. He was a very exuberant man. That morning he was wearing a sport shirt open at the neck and a suede jacket. He always seemed a bit uncomfortable, as if he had just taken too much food or drink. He looked a lot like the old actor Brian Donlevy, right down to his mustache.

They were, to my mind, an incongruous pair, Felix and Alison. On the one hand I felt he had literally stolen her away from me.

But I also realized what a good man he was, and that, given who she might have hooked up with in a city like New York, I had no business complaining about Felix. He rarely talked about his profession: psychiatry. Probably because he wasn't in private practice and most of his psychiatric work consisted of consulting with various accreditation boards as to the training of other psychiatrists. When he bubbled over, which was often, it was invariably about one or another of his collecting manias—Haitian art, fountain pens, Early American quilts, rare coins, and God knows what else. And now, of course, he had collected Alison. But I assumed he was not about to trade her off for an older or more valuable model. When I caught Alison staring at him on more than one occasion with that helplessly dumb, enraptured look, I had to assume that there was more to Felix Drinnan than met the eye. And I knew in my heart, deep down, although I would never admit it, that there was no man Alison could fall in love with that I would approve of. I had, indeed, become the proverbial censurious aunt.

"We're not brunching in the house," Alison replied gaily. "Actually, we're going on a picnic, Auntie."

For that silly mode of addressing me, I chastised her with a little purse of my mouth. "Picnic? What do you mean?"

At that moment Felix pulled out a massive, stuffed wicker hamper that looked as if it had a life as a prop in a Victorian melodrama.

"A picnic?" I asked again. "Really?"

"Really, Aunt Alice."

How strange. The frost was barely off the trees. But I did not protest. We left immediately, climbed into Felix's wine red Lexus, and drove off.

"Are we going to Central Park?" I asked.

"You're not even close," Alison said mischievously.

It wasn't much of a ride. In the wink of an eye we were parking in front of a large, squat blue building on Washington Street, not three minutes away from Felix's place. The building had obviously once been a factory. One could see etched into the brick the remnants of some old industrial hieroglyphics.

Neither Felix nor Alison made a move to leave the car. I looked at my niece in total puzzlement. She only smiled. Then, in a minute, we were all climbing out of the car and slamming the doors locked behind us. Felix led us right to the weird blue building and up the front stairs.

"Felix bought this building five years ago," Alison said casually. "He's done the basic overhauling of it, but he decided to let each tenant do his own renovations. A Chinese furniture designer lives on the ground floor. A drug dealer lives on the second floor—"

"Don't say that, Alison!" Felix had turned and interrupted her sharply. "We don't know what he does for a living. All we know is he has an awful lot of cash."

"Of course, my love," she said in exaggerated concession, and winked at me.

On the third floor we stopped. Felix produced another key, breathing hard from the heft of the picnic basket, and opened a brand-new steel door.

We entered an empty loft with huge windows on all sides. It looked like the industrial space it had once been except for the walls, which had been freshly painted a beautiful peach-tinted white, and the new wooden floor, which had obviously been laid over concrete.

Well, it wasn't *totally* empty. In the center of this massive space was a bridge table and four folding chairs. And in the north corner was a spanking-new refrigerator.

"Please allow me," Felix said, being downright courtly. He pulled out a chair for me. I sat down with equally formal manners. If he wanted to play the gay blade, I was willing to help him out. Then he went to the refrigerator and removed a bottle of very grand champagne. Alison cracked open the hamper. First she removed a gleaming stainless-steel thermos filled with espresso. Then another with some milder blend. Then she pulled out the warm bagels—bagels of every kind—poppy seed, onion, pumpernickel, raisin—and the sweet butter and the cream cheese and the water biscuits and the runny cheeses. And then the caviar! Two beautiful containers of it. And the most luscious assortment of fruits I've ever seen. It was a sumptuous spread.

The windows of the great spacy loft were so large that we literally seemed to be outdoors. The sunlight seemed to negate the walls and the ceiling, where the industrial sprinkler system was still attached.

"I think," I said, "this is the best kind of celebration . . . for both of you." I was sincere. In spite of my problems with his suitability for my niece, and in spite of my unhappiness that she had now basically left my life so quickly after we had found each other, I was very happy for both of them. They were in love. Really in love. And it was only natural to be glad about that.

For no reason at all, Alison burst out laughing then, and stared conspiratorially at Felix. He, too, had a strange look on his face, as if he had swallowed the proverbial canary.

"But you have it all wrong, Aunt Alice. We're not what the celebration is all about."

I was confused and must have looked it.

"You see," Alison continued, "the party isn't for us—it's for you. To celebrate your new apartment."

"I don't have a new apartment."

"Yes, you do. You're sitting in it right now.

This is your new home, Aunt Alice. Rent free."

"Is this some sort of joke?"

"Not at all, Alice," Felix said. "We're absolutely serious. You see, I can't rent the place for the price I want. It's been vacant for ages. The rich think it's a bit too downtown—too *outré*—and the hip don't have enough money. So I decided to take it off the market for a year. Until the economy shakes out. And coincidentally, Alison and I wanted to do something nice for you—to show you how much we appreciated what you've done for her. So . . . here you are. Your new loft. No rent for at least a year. Do whatever you like with it."

"But this is ridiculous, Felix. This is crazy! I can't accept an apartment from you—*a rent-free apartment*—as if it were a box of chocolates."

I simply wouldn't even consider their offer. My mind was made up. People just didn't do things like that. But then . . . then . . . I began to look around more carefully. And I realized this was the stuff that dreams are made of. I knew I could love this place, love living in it. And as for the cats—I just had to look at all those windowsills to imagine how happy being here would make them. No! I had to stop thinking this way. I wouldn't accept it. I couldn't accept it. Except . . . just picturing myself scouring the downtown shops for fabric and furniture and lovely old china made my pulse quicken.

I took a few bites of bagel, trying to remain calm and analytical, as if I were approaching a script. Of course, the freedom from paying rent wouldn't be the only benefit. I'd have a new neighborhood, a new start in the city, maybe all sorts of things in my life would change. *And I'd be living in the Village*, which I had always loved—who didn't?—even if this was the southernmost, westernmost edge of it.

But there was no point in following this line of thought. I wasn't going to accept. It was a generous offer but an insane one. Almost lewd.

And yet . . . here was a way for me to do a good deed for someone else. If I moved in here, Basillio could have my old apartment—for a year or however long I was here. That was a rent even he could afford. And it would give him a rest from hotel rooms, some much needed stability and domesticity. The money I'd save by having no rent to pay, I could use to furnish the loft.

I didn't know what to do. So I kept eating caviar.

Alison, in her attempt to get me to say yes, played shamelessly on the emotional angle and underlined what fun the two of us could have in the neighborhood—only a few blocks away from each other.

I drank more champagne.

Felix outlined the wonders of the loft, getting up from time to time to demonstrate how the shutters worked or to point out the cleverly concealed heating ducts.

Suddenly I realized that I hated this generous man. The hate just bubbled through me. It was such a powerful and unexpected emotion that I closed my eyes and turned away. Felix kept talking. The hatred passed. But from whence had it come? Did I hate him because he was rich and could afford to be generous? Had my many years of financial struggling so poisoned my mind against the affluent that I couldn't accept generosity from them? I looked quickly at Alison. She smiled at me. I smiled back. Then I realized what had happened. This kindly man had enabled my niece to turn the tables on me and I couldn't handle it. I had been the one taking care of her. And now, suddenly, she seemed to be taking care of me. It made me feel like a senior citizen.

I listened to my conscience and to my heart. And in the end, I accepted.

I got up and in a kind of daze wandered around my new loft, a plastic champagne flute in my hand.

A couple of hours later I waltzed up the stairs of the old tenement I'd called home for so many years, and when Bushy and Pancho came to greet me at the apartment door

I picked them up and commenced to tango with them.

I had just about run out of nonsense lyrics for "Jealousy" when I looked over and noticed the blinking red light on the answering machine.

The caller's voice sounded familiar. I knew I'd heard it someplace before. And then he identified himself: Danny Celestino. It took a few seconds for face and voice to coalesce in my memory. He left a phone number. He wanted me to call back immediately—as soon as I got in—whenever I got in.

I was more than a little thrown by the call. Clients were supposed to call the Village Cat People for help—not the other way around. I certainly never expected to have any further dealings with the VCP—didn't want any reminders of the horrible thing that had happened to that young woman from their organization—as if I'd need any reminders. What on earth could they possibly want from me—an endorsement?

And then it hit me: My check must have bounced! I was all but positive I had more than enough in the bank to cover the bill, but I've been wrong before. Chagrined, I picked up the receiver and called the number Celestino had left. He answered on the first ring.

"Hello. This is Alice Nestleton. Did I by any chance—"

"This is really important, Alice. Can we get

together right away—right now? It's *really* important."

For a moment I thought he was making a pass. But then I sobered up. "Get together for what purpose, Danny?"

There was a very long pause on his end of the line. Finally, he said softly, "It's about Martha . . . Lorenz."

No thinking twice about who that name had belonged to. Damn! He had pressed the right button. The guilt button.

"When and where did you want to meet?"

"Right now," he said. "I'm in a cafe on Hudson Street. Near Morton. It's called—"

"It's called Maurizio's."

"Yes. You know the place?"

"I just left the area fifteen minutes ago, Danny."

"Well, jump in a cab. I'll reimburse you."

Reimburse? What a queer way to phrase it. As if I were an underling working for him. Or perhaps it was just the lingo of a new generation of arrogant, out-of-work actors.

"Okay, you two," I told the cats. "Later." But I didn't move out the front door immediately. I hesitated, lingering over my good-bye scratches behind the ears of the pusses.

I did get out of the door, though, and headed down the endless stairs, but with nothing like the spirit I'd shown coming up.

4

It was a lovely little coffee place, if a bit cramped. Danny was not alone. Two women—one on either side of him—sat at the small table, too. All three looked extremely tense, expectant. I hadn't the slightest idea what was going on. But the mood was dreadful—as if a closing notice had just been posted.

I ordered a cappuccino. Danny Celestino introduced the two women—Ann Walters and Libby Trask—as his coworkers at Village Cat People. Ann had beautiful gray eyes and wore an old-fashioned pinafore. Libby was tall and willowy, like a fashion model. Both could very well have been out-of-work performers.

"Thank you for coming, Alice," Danny said, but it was more in the way of a proclamation for the others. Then he leaned forward until he was only an inch or two away from my face. The two girls leaned forward with him. "You know, Alice—or Miss Nestleton—whatever you'd like to be called—we've heard about your work."

I smiled. "Well, when you've been in the theater as long as I have, sooner or later a few people hear of you . . . happily."

Libby Trask fairly hissed in response: "We're not talking about the theater, Miss Nestleton. We're talking about your other activities. Crime."

I was flabbergasted. As far as I knew, I was hardly a household word as a criminal investigator.

"We need your help," Danny said pleadingly.

"Yes. We need it bad," affirmed Ann Walters, who was now holding on to the sugar dispenser as if it were a life raft.

Danny spoke again, carefully articulating every syllable in every word: "Martha Lorenz was not killed by any street criminal. She was assassinated. It was a cold-blooded, premeditated murder made to look like a mugging that got out of hand."

It was such a jolting statement that for the longest time I didn't know what to do or how to reply. I just kept sipping my cappuccino, staring from one of my tortured young hosts to another, searching for some sign of drunkenness. But they weren't drunk. They sat there stoically waiting for my response.

"Those are some very strong assertions," I

said at last. "Do you have any proof to back them up?"

Danny said, the passion rising, "A week before it happened Martha told all of us she was marked for death. In those words. She said she was being hunted. We asked her who would want to kill her. She was wonderful, Marty. Full of life, kind, open. Everybody loved her. Of course we couldn't believe anyone would want to hurt her."

I waited. When he didn't finish the story, I prompted, "Yes? . . . What did she answer when you asked who was hunting her down?"

"She wouldn't tell us," he said. "All she said was a single word, as if that was enough to explain it all."

"And the word was . . .?"

"An Italian word. At least it sounded Italian. My grandparents came from Italy but I don't speak a word of the language."

Libby took a napkin from the table dispenser and proceeded to letter a word on it with her ballpoint pen. When she was done she pushed the napkin over to me.

ASPETTANDO

"This was Martha's answer?"

"That's what it sounded like to us," Ann said. "I can't vouch for the spelling."

"Do you have a quarter?" I asked.

Libby produced one, handed it to me. I

walked to the pay phone a few feet away from the table and called Basillio.

"Tony, it's me. I need some information."

"How dare you interrupt my creative process for mere information?"

"What is it that you're creating?"

"I'll tell you, Swede. I am conceiving a spectacular stage design for the next revival of *Guys and Dolls*. They'll be reviving that thing as long as there's a Broadway, so I figure they'll use my stuff on the next go-around. It will consist only of an enormous feed bag."

"Why a feed bag?"

"Because horse racing is central to the—if you'll pardon the expression—plot. Everyone's always betting on horses in that show. There are even songs about it."

"You have a point, Tony. It may be an idiotic one, but a point nonetheless. But tell me, what does the Italian word *aspettando* mean?" I spelled it for him.

"It means what is always going on between you and me."

"Which is?"

"Waiting . . . the process of waiting. Could be for something good or could be for something bad. All you know is it's going to be intense. But you wait for it to happen."

"I see. Well, thanks. Listen, Tony, I've got . . . never mind for now. I'll talk to you later."

I was going to tell him right then about

the new loft on Washington Street, but at the last moment I lost courage. I hung up and walked back to the table.

"Does that clarify anything?" I asked the three young people after passing on my version of Basillio's explanation.

They shook their heads. They didn't seem disappointed, though. Perhaps they hadn't expected clarification.

Libby Trask said bluntly, "We want you to conduct the investigation."

"What investigation?"

"Of Martha's murder, of course. We want you to find out who did it."

"Look. The police are conducting their own very intensive investigation, I'm sure. Why don't you go to them with this information? It isn't much, but maybe it will help."

"Don't you understand? They're convinced she was killed by a mugger," Danny said contemptuously.

"Then you'll have to persuade them otherwise," I said with equal force. "Tell them everything you've just told me. Maybe you can make them change their minds about it. But, to be honest, I don't think they will."

"But why won't you help us? Why?" Ann's voice was full of pain.

I sat back in my chair. Why, indeed, didn't I want to help them? I didn't know. After all, Martha Lorenz had died ringing my doorbell—she was there to help me. And, if I was right about these good-looking youngsters,

we were all out-of-work theater people. I
had become involved in murder in the past
on connections a lot flimsier than this one.
Perhaps it was because in my heart I believed Martha had indeed been killed by a
common thief and nothing her friends had
told me had changed my view even a tiny
bit. Or perhaps I was just too excited, dis-
tracted, by the promise of a new place to
live.

"Listen, all of you. Please. Go to the police
and tell them your story. You've asked for
my advice and that is the best advice I can
give you."

"All right," Ann said. "We'll go. But could
you at least come to Martha's apartment
with us first?"

"Why?"

They looked at one another. No one answered my simple question. Then I realized
that they were frightened to go alone. Not
frightened in the sense of being fearful for
their personal safety, but frightened of entering the domain of the dead. My grandmother once told me that after her husband
died, my grandfather, she could not bring
herself to step into their bedroom again for
three years.

"Sure," I said.

Danny paid the check.

Martha had lived in a crumbling tenement
on Jane Street, two floors above an old Village landmark of a bar. I could recall being

taken there for drinks by one of the first
young men I dated after moving to New
York.

I stood just inside the doorway of the
small apartment while the three young people scurried about. It was obvious they were
looking for something that would confirm
their beliefs about how Martha died—something to impress me—a diary, a letter, a clue
of some sort. They seemed to be finding
nothing at all. Well, that isn't exactly true.
They did find heartache. They began to
stare at familiar objects, at pieces of
Martha's clothing, a coffee cup on the
kitchen table, a magazine left in the arm-
chair. The little apartment was overwhelm-
ing them.

Finally they all began to file out. I was
damn relieved it was coming to an end.

"Wait!" Libby called out in the craziest
kind of staccato voice. We all halted in our
tracks.

"Look!" She stood pointing at one spot on
the wall and then another, pointing, it
seemed, at absolutely nothing. All we saw
were the picture frames hung here and
there on the walls. "Look, damn it! They're
empty," Libby said. "Look at them. They're
all empty!"

The rest of us took a collective step back
and followed where Libby pointed on the
wall. She was right. Someone had removed

the objects from every frame but left the frames themselves undisturbed.

"What was in those frames?" I asked.

They stood there looking at one another, trying to recall, and then back at the wall.

"She used to have stuff about the Village," Danny said.

"Yes," Libby added. "Antique maps. I remember at least one old map of Greenwich Village in one of these frames."

"And photographs," said Ann. "Old photographs of artists and writers who had lived and worked in the Village. You know, Eugene O'Neill and John Reed, and people like that."

"The Village when it was bohemian," Libby said.

"Were those things worth money?" I asked.

None of them could answer that question.

"Are you sure they were taken after Martha was killed? Could she have removed them herself for some reason? I mean, perhaps she was planning to paint soon."

They were again at a loss. They just kept staring at the empty frames. And they didn't look so young anymore. They looked older and tireder and too washed out to make any more house calls.

"Look," I said, "just make sure to tell the police about this, too. Maybe it is significant."

"Everything's significant," Danny retorted.

Well, there seemed little doubt about it now—he was an actor all right. I almost smiled at him like an indulgent parent.

We locked up the place and headed down the steep stairs.

I was tired, too, but not as downhearted as I knew my companions were. I could only wish them luck in their dealings with the police. And I could only hope they would come to terms with the loss of their friend and colleague.

But I had no reason for unhappiness: I was about to embark on a great new phase of my life. It was all I could do not to run down the steps ahead of them all.

5

Two days later (a Tuesday)—with two helpers (Tony and Alison)—two cats (Bushy and Pancho)—two overstuffed valises (the wardrobe)—and two shopping bags (one containing cosmetics, sundries, and personal papers; the other a starter set of tinned goods and such for the pantry)—I took up residence in my magnificent new Washington Street loft.

I released the disoriented cats and watched them scurry away, searching in vain for a hiding place in the wide open room.

"I think you may have overlooked one small detail," Tony said, surveying the room.

"What do you mean?" I said.

"What are you going to sleep on?"

I smiled and instanteously unfurled the spartan pallet I'd been carrying under my arm.

"You must be kidding," Tony snorted. "You can't sleep on that little napkin."

"Of course I'm going to sleep on it—until I find the perfect bed."

"You're getting a little carried away with this start-from-scratch business, aren't you, Swede?"

"I think he may have a point, Aunt Alice," Alison put in. "Why don't you let Felix give you that daybed from one of the spare rooms—just temporarily. Or at least accept his offer to get a carpenter in here to build a platform for you. He could be here by the end of the day."

I didn't answer. I wasn't interested. I was watching Bushy, who had leapt up onto one of the windowsills and seemed to be stretching his entire Maine coon body into contortions in the unaccustomed light. Soon, I knew, Pancho would start zooming from window to window, wall to wall, because there was no doubt in his mind, nor in mine, that his secret enemies followed him wherever he went.

"Look, Swede, I can bring over some stuff for you every few days. After all, I'm going to be living in your apartment."

"And paying the rent, Tony," I reminded him. "Every month. On time."

"Yeah yeah yeah."

"*On time.* Remember, Tony. But as for the things I've left over there . . . just leave them. I told you, I want to leave the Twenty-sixth Street place intact. This space is my new beginning. Understand?"

Alison opened the bag that held the containers of coffee she had purchased at the Lost Diner, a bustling coffee shop on West Street that was the last outpost of civilization before you hit the Hudson River. I heard a crinkling of wax paper and saw that she was also unwrapping some really attractive buttered corn muffins.

We snapped open three red metal chairs and seated ourselves at the folding table. It was almost noon. I had opened a few of the windows at the top and a delicious breeze was playing through the loft. No one spoke for a few moments. There was something in the room with us: the spirit of spring. You could almost taste it on your tongue.

We heard a ship's whistle from the nearby river.

"This place is going to get mighty dusty if you leave those windows open," Tony cautioned.

The thought of Basillio wielding a feather duster was a funny one. I leaned over suddenly and kissed him. He looked very confused. I suppose Alison was, too; she gave us one of her crooked half smiles. Bushy decided to join us just then. I wouldn't allow him to forage on the tabletop, but I did agree to his sitting in Alison's lap, from which he could poke around discreetly and lick the butter from the discarded muffin wrappings.

"You know, Swede," Tony noted, "this loft is big enough for a legitimate theater."

"The neighbors may not like that," Alison said.

"I thought there were only two other tenants in the building," Tony said. "A drug dealer and a designer. Forget about them."

Tony was on his feet, outlining for us his grand design for a loft theater when we heard a most ungodly sound. It was like a claxon horn fused with a cowbell, and it shook the fillings in my teeth.

"Don't worry," Alison assured us. "It's only the downstairs bell. Someone wants to get in. Felix said he'd have that sound adjusted; I guess it just slipped his mind. But let me show you how to ring people in."

I followed her to the loft door. And then just outside. For some reason the response buzzer had been put on the outside of the door. But no matter. Just like 26th Street, I pressed the button, held it down for a count of five, then waited to see who was climbing up the stiars.

"Alice Nestleton?" he called out—whoever "he" was.

"Yes. Who is it?"

Danny Celestino came into view then, and like his twin shadows, Ann and Libby came climbing after.

I was astonished to see them. And not

very happy. How did they even know I had moved to the Village? And, most important, what did they want now?

"May we come up?" Libby asked. "We got your new address from a neighbor in your old building . . . a Mrs. Oshrin."

I didn't answer right away. I had no wish to be rude, but . . .

"Who are those people?" Alison said delicately behind my ear.

"May I introduce," I said a little too loudly, "the Village Cat People."

Alison shrank back into the apartment, thinking, no doubt, about Martha Lorenz.

The three of them were now virtually in the doorway to the apartment. My astonishment was rapidly turning to anger. But then another surprise came along to dissipate it. Out of the open door ambled crazy Pancho. He walked right over to Danny and began to rub against his leg for all he was worth. This was the stranger who had trapped him, manhandled him, jammed a needle into him. My big old gray alley cat was begging for his affection, purring like a kitten. Unbelievable! Danny bent down and gave Pancho a couple of peremptory strokes behind the ear.

If Pancho was trying to shame me into being civil to the uninvited guestss, he succeeded. I gestured the young people over the threshold and through the door and then introduced them properly, each by name, to

Alison and Tony. We all hovered around the single folding table. Tony had already met Danny, of course, but not the two girls. His eyes were gleaming like stars in the night sky as he shook hands with Libby Trask. Basillio had always been partial to long-limbed young beauties. I felt a sudden twinge. I, in fact, had been just such a leggy young beauty. Indeed, a notoriously nasty critic had once written that my performance in the very serious second effort by what turned out to be a one-play genius was nothing short of "criminally wacky"—but he recommended the play highly, because I spent most of my time onstage in shorts and halter.

Not that I think of myself now as a thing too grotesque to look upon. Not at all. It's just that when people talk about me now, I suspect they describe me in terms no more rhapsodic than "a tall, nice-looking blonde."

It was Ann Walters who blurted out: "We followed your suggestion, Miss Nestleton. We went to the police. We told them everything we told you. They essentially called us fools. Oh, they weren't nasty about it. But they patronized us severely."

Libby interjected passionately. "We don't have anyone else to turn to. You've got to help us."

Alison and Tony were baldly staring, not at the two young women, but at me. And there was accusation and incredulity in

their eyes—as if I were evil, as if I were with-
holding sustenance from a child.

"Look," I said, directly to my niece, "they
want me to investigate the death of that
young woman in my lobby. They're convinced
that she was . . . assassinated. That the robbery was faked. And they have precious little
to back up their claims. *Not* precious little—
nothing. Believe me. I'm telling you . . ."

But Tony and Alison did not moderate
their gaze.

Then Danny thrust a piece of paper into
my hand, with force, as if the paper would
singe him if he held it too long.

"What is this?" I asked wearily.

"We got together, the three of us, and tried
to reconstruct what had been in every picture frame on the wall. You remember—the
frames that someone—"

"Yes, Danny, I remember. Go on."

"We tried our best to remember all the
stuff she had hanging up. We don't know
how accurate we were. But we made an attempt."

I put the paper on top of the table next to
a coffee container and uncrinkled it.

I didn't read the list. I never got past the
first item:

PHOTOGRAPH OF EDNA ST. VINCENT MILLAY

I was suddenly overwhelmed by nostal-
gia. Was it the same photograph I had had

in my room, growing up? I could remember that photo clearly—a lovely young woman—the fierce wish to live to the fullest already there in her eyes. Was it that photograph? Taken around 1915, when she was about twenty . . . when she entered Vassar College on a scholarship after attending Barnard, in New York, for about six months?

Had Edna St. Vincent Millay meant the same things to Martha Lorenz she had meant to me, twenty-five years ago? Millay had personified everything good to me . . . everything beautiful . . . everything free. Maybe Martha Lorenz had been the same kind of restless, yearning girl-woman I had been.

I knew they were all looking at me—the Cat People and Alison and Tony—but I didn't care. The words from one of Millay's best-known poems seemed to be knocking in my ears, but I couldn't remember them exactly . . . something about burning the candle at both ends . . . a candle that represented the freedom of wild, bohemian Greenwich Village . . . that will not survive the night of passion. *It makes a lovely light!*

I moved swiftly away from the table and turned my back to the others. Tony came up behind me and touched my shoulder. "What is it?"

I shook him off and turned to the Village Cat People. "All right," I said. "I will help you. I will investigate the murder of your friend Martha."

6

Detective Vargas sat uncomfortably on a folding chair. It was early morning. He was here in the loft only as a begrudging favor to one Lieutenant Rothwax, who had been my mentor and friend at RETRO during my short and very unhappy tenure there as a consultant for the New York Police Department. I had called Rothwax and asked him to intercede; told him I wished to speak with one of the detectives working on the Martha Lorenz case. Rothwax had set it up.

For some reason, Bushy found Vargas fascinating and kept circling the portly, well-dressed police officer. The cat nudged the detective's calves with his nose; he picked at his shoelaces; he sniffed at his thin black socks, and even stood on his back legs making soulful eyes at Vargas. But to no avail. The detective never paid a minute's attention to old Bushy.

I pushed the list across the table. Vargas picked it up gingerly and began to read from it in stentorian tones, as if there were an audience present. But there was no one except him and me, and the two cats, of course. Tony had said he intended to sleep late this morning. My move had exhausted him even more than it had me. And the lovestruck Alison had been spending happy mornings, full of lazy lovemaking, I was guessing, with Felix, who had taken a few days off from work.

So who could know when either of them would show? Vargas was there, so I proceeded alone even though it was Alison's and Tony's silent contempt for my orginal investigative "nay," which had transformed it into an "aye."

"Photo of Edna Saint Vincent Millay

Photo of MacDougal Street at a time it was working-class Italian

Several old programs from the Provincetown Players

Several photos of beautiful Greenwich Village town houses

Reproduction of hand-drawn and -lettered street map of Greenwich Village, pre-World War I

Menu from a Village restaurant, circa 1922

Poster of *Masses* magazine cover dated 1919."

Vargas raised his eyebrows after he finished reading the list, lay the paper facedown on the table, and pushed it back toward me.

"All this stuff was on her wall? And it was all stolen?"

"No. Her three associates wrote down what *might* have been on the wall. Items they remembered associated with Martha Lorenz. None of them remembered exactly what was hanging where. But at least we know eight frames were looted."

"Any of it worth anything?"

"I don't know."

He sighed greatly and leaned over the table as if he were confiding in me. "This is one of the most cut-and-dried cases I ever saw. Classic push-in mugging that went bad. He sees her packages. Sees her enter a building. He figures she lives there. He takes whatever she has. We got a partial description of a loiterer on your block. We haven't got the knife yet. In most cases the knife is thrown away immediately."

"You don't think there's any possibility that her friends' claim is correct: that she was tracked down and murdered?"

"For what? Who'd want to kill a harmless kook like her? Give me some names and motives."

"What about this very strange theft in her apartment—no jewelry stolen, typewriter left alone, clock radio, and so on, but they steal the rather esoteric memorabilia from the walls. All of which is strange enough in itself; but to make matters worse, they leave the frames. What do you make of it, Detective?"

"All I can say, lady, stranger things have happened. A person dies, neighbors come in and loot the place. A typewriter and a radio, they already got. But maybe it just so happens that stuff on the wall was exactly the kind of art somebody else in the building was interested in—always envious of the dead girl because she found it before they did. Who knows? Maybe even one of those three friends of hers really stole the stuff and the other two don't know about it. Anything's possible."

"Hmm. I suppose you could be right, Detective Vargas. And what about what Martha Lorenz told the others before she died?"

"You mean about somebody being after her."

"That's right."

He leaned back in the chair very daintily, as if he knew the folding chair could collapse at any minute. Vargas clasped his hands behind his head. He suddenly looked very wise. "I don't know what to tell you about that. Maybe she owed money. People in debt often think somebody's following them. Maybe she was fooling around with a married guy and thought the wife had found out. You never know—there're a hundred maybe's." He stopped talking abruptly and looked around the apartment, as if seeing it for the first time.

"You *live* here?"

"Yes," I said, a little defensively. "I'm in the process of furnishing it."

"Oh. . . . Well, good luck."

He was gone five minutes later, after we had engaged in the obligatory dialogue about how wonderful Lieutenant Rothwax was—the exemplary cop—despite his legendary sharp tongue and quick temper.

After Detective Vargas left, Bushy seemed to become morose. Not even the tuna treats I offered him could pick up his spirits. Either, like Pancho, he had become wildly attached to a visitor who had little interest in him, or the wide open spaces and the endless light in the loft were unhinging him.

I realized, of course, that I had set up the detective's visit here because, while I had agreed to help the Village Cat People, I hadn't the slightest idea how to proceed. What had Vargas told me that I didn't already know? Nothing. I had called in a favor from Rothwax and taken up Detective Vargas's time for no good reason. After he left, I realized also, to my chagrin, that I hadn't even offered him a cup of coffee.

I began to circumnavigate my new dwelling, slowly, staring out each tremendous window: west to the Hudson River through some industrial buildings; south to the Twin Towers of the World Trade Center; east to the lovely little streets that bisected wide Hudson; only to the north was there a stingy view, blocked by a massive new office building that housed publishing companies, printing plants, a supermarket, and a few wealthy vagabonds.

I felt guilty as hell about it, but my heart wasn't in the Martha Lorenz investigation. I just didn't have the requisite concentration. My thoughts kept going away from Martha and the VCP, focusing instead on the loft. So many ideas for furnishing it were popping into my consciousness that I felt like a Conran's catalog. Pancho zoomed past me, onto a far ledge. The blur of his fast-moving body brought me back to business. If I wanted to get on to decorating the loft, I had to end this business with the Cat People. I neither believed them nor disbelieved them, but I had to go through the paces with some kind of dedication and verve. Get hold of yourself, Alice, I said. Take hold. Get cracking. I had to focus on some of the basics: Who did the young woman love and hate? Who loved and who hated her?

The best place to start answering these questions, I knew, was in that little apartment on Jane Street.

I was trying to look sharp. But just to be sure, I brought along three other pairs of eyes. Alison and Tony as well as Libby

Trask came with me. It surely was a small apartment. You entered the place and immediately faced the door to a tiny bathroom. The high-ceilinged hallway led to the main room. Off of that was a kitchen for Munchkins—a truncated refrigerator sitting beneath a range—hardly enough room to extend both your arms. Built-in cabinets reached halfway to the ceiling.

I went back to the hallway and counted the empty frames on the wall. There were eight of them.

Then we began the search in earnest. "Look for anything with a name on it—business cards, books, mail, anything." Those were my instructions to the troops. And they carried them out with a vengeance.

Only Tony found anything of interest. He brought it to me and I set it on the coffee table. We all gathered around it. It was an oversized wooden file box.

"Probably her recipe file," Alison speculated.

I opened the box. Inside were tabbed separators, twelve of them. On each tab was printed the name of a street in the Village, in alphabetical order: Bank, Barrow, Bedford, Charles, Jane, Perry, and so on.

But, whatever had been filed between the separators—in other words, the real "meat" of the box, the "hard information"—was gone.

"Do you recognize this?" I asked Libby. "Any idea what she was doing with it?"

She shook her head.

I ventured some baseless speculation of my own. "I guess it's possible that the person who removed the items from the frames also removed the index cards from this box."

"But it's so small," Tony said. "Why not take the whole damn file?"

"I don't know," I admitted.

"Maybe," Alison suggested, "nothing's been taken from the box. Maybe Martha was only *thinking* of starting some sort of project. Like writing a book about Greenwich Village. Or cataloging all her memorabilia about the Village—something like that. Perhaps she was going to make a list of things she would like to buy or sell, so that she could advertise in a collector's magazine. Felix has lists like that on his computer, but it's the same principle."

"That's very good, Alison," I said.

"Yeah, but why would she collect or file by street name?" Tony said. "It doesn't make sense. You organize that kind of stuff by year or by genre or by the name of the person who created it—anything but the street."

Then I found another separator at the back of the box. The name "Bruno" was lettered on it.

This "file" actually contained something— two postcards. The kind of nicely reproduced art postcards one could buy in the gift shop of any museum. One card reproduced Poussin's famous painting *The Rape of the Sabine Women*. The other card was Rubens's painting on the same theme.

"Did Martha ever talk about a man named Bruno?" I asked Libby.

"No, not that I recall."

"What about these cards? Do they mean anything to you?"

"Not a thing."

I sat straight up in my chair then. "Wait a minute! What if Bruno is a cat?"

"That's possible," Libby agreed.

"Or maybe Bruno is the name of a person whose cat Martha took care of."

"That's *very* possible," Libby said, then added, "and it's very easy to check, because we keep logs."

"Logs of what?"

"Of all the house calls we make. Since most visits are one-person affairs, and we often get called again and again to see the same animal, we need to have information on the cat in some central place, so that any of us has easy access to it. After each visit, we write down the owner's name and address, the date, the cat's name, the problem, and how it was resolved, the fee charged—things like that."

"Where are the logs kept?"

"In the office."

"Tell me, Libby: Martha was a very pretty

young woman, but none of you have talked about the men in her life. Were there many? . . . Were there any?"

"None that I know of. She didn't talk about that sort of thing. Do you think this Bruno was her lover—or ex-lover?—something like that?"

"Maybe it's the name of a sauce," Tony offered.

All eyes turned to him. Not one of us laughed. A man showing off in front of a pretty woman must be one of the saddest things on earth.

"I wouldn't want to guess about Bruno just yet," I told Libby. "First I need to get a look at those logs. Where exactly is the office?"

"On Morton Street, just west of Bleecker. In the basement of the first house in from the corner. There's a sign on the iron rail. You can't miss us."

7

It was close to noon. The Cafe Vivaldi, on Jones Street, had just opened. Tony and I were seated inside, waiting for Alison. She was late. We were supposed to meet at 11:30 and then all go across the street to the world headquarters of the Village Cat People to examine Martha Lorenz's log book. In spite of the possibly rifled index card file in her apartment and the strange emergence of someone or something called Bruno, I still had little enthusiasm for the investigation. It was simply something I should do, given the circumstances.

Alison swept in at 12:15. She looked flushed and radiant and absolutely beautiful, with her golden bobbed hair and peaches and cream complexion. Wearing an expensive raw silk chemise, she looked like a Minnesota milkmaid who had gone straight from the farm to the pages of *Vogue* magazine. Of course, Alison had never even been on my grandmother's farm.

"Nice of you to join us," Tony muttered in her direction.

I don't think she even heard him. My niece sat down and grabbed my hand. A torrent of words rushed out. "I can't spend the day with you, Aunt Alice. Felix is driving me to Quogue. To see Piaf!"

"I don't know how to break this to you, Alison," Tony said, "but Piaf's been dead about forty years."

She ignored the remark. "The lawyer from Dorothy Dodd's estate called this morning. Her highness Piaf is temporarily domiciled in someplace called Quogue. And I can visit her, he said."

"That's wonderful, dear," I said. "Tony, you know about Piaf—Maud, that is. Each one of that little cat's ears is worth about ten million dollars."

"Oh," Tony replied dully. "The French cat caper." Tony tended to refer dismissively to my time in France, where I'd been reunited—or rather united for the first time—with my niece. "Why is everybody so caught up—"

"Later, Tony," I interrupted. "Later."

"Where is this Quogue?" Alison asked.

"It's a posh little town on the ocean, just before you get to the Hamptons. Great Gatsby country," Basillio piped up.

"Then it's not so far away?"

"Two or three hours by car," he said. Then he added, "You know, Alison, you always seem to gravitate toward money."

I kicked him under the table, hard. Alison reddened and retorted in a soft but passionate voice, "I love Felix in spite of his money, not because of it."

The smirk on Basillio's face was almost too much to bear. I was going to kick him again, but I thought better of it. After all, I needed his help even more now, if Alison was not going to be around.

She stood up, kissed me hurriedly on the cheek, and with a backward wave of her hand ran toward the cafe door.

"Say hello to Piaf from me," I reminded her.

Then I turned on Tony. "That was an incredibly stupid, rude thing you said to her."

"Well, ever since you got back from Europe, the two of you have been acting like some dotty old broads. I mean, who cares that some cat is worth a billion dollars."

"Look, Tony, I've explained to you that Alison doesn't love that cat because of the money. It's all tied up with the past . . . her husband and their life together."

He shook his head and slumped in his chair. The waitress delivered his espresso. He just glared at it.

"You're sulking like a little boy, Tony. What is the matter with you?"

"No," he snapped. "The question should be, what's the matter with *you*?"

"You never liked Alison. But at least, up to now, you were able to be civil to her."

"That's not true. It's just that since she came back with you, everything has gone haywire. She was always around. All your attention was focused on her. And then, finally, she falls in love and moves out, and I think we can spend some time together. But no. Her rich boyfriend just hands you this airplane hangar of an apartment. You move out of the old place and now we're farther apart than ever. Which seems just fine to you. In addition, you're acting so goddamn strange recently I just don't know how to deal with you, Swede."

I took a deep breath. I didn't want to fight with him. We had work to do.

"I'm not acting strange, Tony. I'm just tired. Can't you understand that? My cat-sitting business is running down. I don't get any referrals. I'm broke. And I haven't been able to land any kind of acting jobs recently. Don't you see that, after miraculously finding my sister's child and then having her with me for such a short time, she's decided to move out. It's like she's leaving me again. All these things are pressing in on me right now. But things will change. You'll see."

"No, it's more than that, Swede. You're starting to sound like a middle-aged lady.

You don't react to things anymore. You don't see things."

I waved a threatening finger at him. "You're treading on dangerous ground, Tony. Give me some examples or kindly keep your mouth shut."

"All right. I'll give you an example: You don't even recognize this place."

"What place?"

"This coffee shop. The Vivaldi."

"Are you crazy? Of course I know this cafe. I've been here before."

"But something else happened here. Think."

I had no idea what he was talking about.

"Drawing a blank?"

I let my eyes roam around. It was the same lovely, cool cafe I remembered—comfortable chairs, large tables, a fireplace, windows onto the street. Three or four outdoor tables for the nice weather. A big glass cabinet displaying the pastries. A high counter behind which the sandwiches were prepared. Bottles of Italian soda and sparkling water on the shelves.

"Don't you remember the Russians, Swede?"

"The Russians?"

"Those three crazed old men. The refugees from the Moscow Art Theatre."

"My God!" A flood of memories came back. Yes, they had met here in this cafe. They had hatched a murderous plot here. And they had considered themselves the guardians of Stanislavski's cats—the white cats they had brought to this country from the Soviet Union.

"You're right, Tony; I'd forgotten. I'm sorry." I understood his hurt some, because that was the first case he had really helped me out on. Without him, nothing would have been achieved.

He looked as if he thought my admission had vindicated him. Basillio squeezed my hand gently and then picked up his espresso.

Perhaps, I thought, I am beginning to act like a self-satisfied middle-aged woman, no longer open to the nuances, to events, to feelings.

Tony finished his coffee in one macho gulp. "Well, boss," he said, sighing contendedly, "ready to go to work?"

We paid our check and left the cafe.

The Village Cat People were right around the corner.

The place was more like an urban root cellar than an office. It was in a basement and there were high windows so that one could see the feet of the passersby. Not only was the office small, it was jammed with equipment—splints, bandages, syringes, cardboard carriers, even cat toys—all kinds of things related to feline medical emergencies.

And the phones, three of them, jangled like madmen, answered by whomever was close. On the walls were slogans like WRITE IT DOWN . . . KITTY DIED FOR YOUR SINS . . . and the like.

The VCP had a single vehicle, and when all three of them were in the small office— Danny, Ann, and Libby—they had to keep an ever watchful eye on the double-parked jeep outside. As Ann told us, it had been towed at least seven times in the last year.

The atmosphere was so chaotic that I soon realized Tony and I would not be able to work there. Libby gave us Martha's ledger, an old-fashioned Bartleby the Scrivener affair complete with worn cloth jacket, and Tony and I walked back to the cafe with it.

I staked claim to a window table and opened the tome. Written across the top of each page were the headings: NAME OF CLIENT; ADDRESS AND PHONE; DATE OF CONTACT; DATE OF VISIT; PROBLEM; DIS-POSITION; FEE.

Each page in the ledger constituted a single day. There were six or seven entries per day. The recordkeeping system was simple and comprehensive—except for one very important aspect: the name of the cat was not recorded, only the name of the paying human client. So, if I were looking for a cat named Bruno, I wouldn't find it in this book.

That was strange: Libby had told us the name of every client's pet was listed. She had not told the truth. Was that simply a memory lapse or had she deliberately lied?

I was particularly fascinated by the "problem" column, which stated why the VCP were called upon or referred by a vet. I saw the last set of statistics poor Martha had noted—mine. It said under that column: Carrier problems. I knew immediately what that meant. Pancho could not be put into his carrier. There was no entry for the "Disposition" or "Fee" column, because Martha had been murdered before she disposed of the problem. It probably, I figured, was recorded in Danny Celestino's log book.

It was good to learn that many of the Village Cat People's visits were "carrier" related. And many had to do with "kitty up a drainpipe" type problems, where the cat had got itself in some awful, freak predicament and needed help extricating himself. It was the kind of problem that people used to call the fire department for. Maybe they still do if they don't know about the Cat People. Other kinds of problems common to the VCP were: inoculating kittens, particularly strays; assisting at difficult births; reviving felines who had lost consciousness; searching for lost cats; dealing with felines who had suddenly begun to exhibit psychotic or destructive symptoms, such as attacking their

owners or smashing all the flowerpots on
the terrace.

I swung the ledger around so that Tony
could read it. He seemed happy to get his
hands on it, turning the pages with great
relish.

"If we take the last two weeks of entries in
Martha's book and check them all out,
that's going to be too many visits for us to
make," I noted.

"Let's phone them instead of trying to
make in-person visits," Tony suggested. "If
anything interesting comes up, then we can
make a house call." He sat back suddenly
and laughed at his own words. "By the way,
Swede, what am I looking for when I speak
to the clients?"

"Two things, Tony. First, a cat named
Bruno. Or a person with that name. And
second, anything the client knew about
Martha's Greenwich Village memorabilia
collecting. Maybe she once admired a photo
or a piece of art in a client's home. Maybe
they had a conversation about collecting
photographs—something like that. It doesn't
seem very promising, but what else have we
got?"

"It suddenly dawns on me, Swede, that we
ought to get Felix as a consultant," Tony
suggested.

"Why Felix?"

"Well, he's the only real collector you
know!"

I laughed. "Tony, listen. Felix is one of those rich people who talks a good game about the beauty of his quilts and coins. But it's really about money. Get it? And one thing I know in my heart is that those things poor Martha collected were not about money. The photo of Edna Saint Vincent Millay she had on her wall probably cost her five dollars. It cost me $1.95 in Minnesota twenty years ago."

"But you ripped it out of a book, didn't you?"

"Let's concentrate on the matter at hand, Tony. Okay? The phone calls."

"We could go up and make the calls from your apartment," he suggested.

"You mean *your* apartment, Basillio. Or were you talking about the loft?"

"It doesn't matter. I have a better idea. A brilliant idea. We'll go to the bank around the corner and get quarters, and then we'll go to the Film Forum on Houston."

"The Film Forum is a movie house."

"I know. But they've got two beautiful pay phones, side by side. And they've also got great bathrooms. And a little coffee place in the lobby, where you buy the popcorn and three-dollar carrot cake. There are a couple of those high counters where you can stand, but no seats. I love that place. It's almost like a bar."

"I see. Look, Tony, we've got work to do."

"No, this is ingenious, Swede. We'll go in

the lobby as if we're waiting for a movie. There are three of them playing at any one time. I think they have a fifties gangster film festival running. We order a coffee or something and stand at the table, relaxing. Then one of us goes to the pay phone and makes three or four calls. Then comes back. Then the other goes. Like a relay. We'll be fresh all the time. Like runners."

I stared at him. More of Tony's unfathomable ways. He had to find ways to put excitement into his life. This was an elaborate, very bizarre plan—a lot of trouble for a few phone calls. Well, a lot of phone calls. But, on the other hand, it might have been all for the best to get this task done in public. No distractions.

"And, Swede," he went on, "if we get weary we'll go into one of the movies. Or we'll go across the street to that down-home place and get some booze and ribs."

"Ribs! Since when do you eat ribs, Basillio?"

"In spring. In the spring my fancy turns to soul food."

"Really, Basillio!" I clucked my tongue. I took the ledger back from him, shut it with a snap, and reflected for a moment. "Tony, I hope this scheme with the pay phones isn't one of your elaborate tricks to get me to see a movie with you—one I don't want to see."

"Who me? Am I that devious?"

I did not answer. We left the cafe and

walked the few blocks to the movie, or rather, to the lobby of the movie house.

Just before we made our first call, we agreed that our "cover" was that we simply wanted the clients to tell us whether or not they had been happy with the services the Village Cat People had provided. If not, why not? Could they elaborate? And the purpose of this follow-up was to make the VCP more efficient.

So there we stood, at one of the counters in the lobby of the trendy downtown revival house, drinking Cokes and making tracks to and from the pay phones. The process was always the same: One or the other of us made three successive calls and then returned to report our findings; then the other made his three calls.

No one in the movie house seemed to find anything out of the ordinary in our behavior. In fact, the other phone was kept pretty busy as well by people looking for work, leaving messages for friends, responding to apartment-for-rent ads, and so on. It was all quite cheery and comradely there in the lobby. And it made me wonder whether there was anyone at all actually in any one of the theaters, watching a film.

We worked like a well-oiled machine, making almost ninety calls in less than two hours. We took notes occasionally, but there wasn't much to write down.

Thirty-four of the clients could not be

reached; either a machine picked up or there was no answer at all. I thought of all the cats sitting alone in those apartments, listening to the ringing.

Forty-one of the clients answered. Of those, thirty-three said they were quite satisfied with the services and would call the Village Cat People again if the need arose. Eight said they were unhappy with the service and would not use the Cat People again. Not one of the forty-one clients had a cat named Bruno or had anyone in their household with the name Bruno. Nor had any of them ever discussed Village memorabilia, collecting photographs, or anything of the sort with Martha Lorenz. Almost half of the respondents did not remember Martha's name.

And fourteen people could not be reached because the number Martha wrote down for them either was the incorrect number or the phone had been disconnected.

Everything had gone beautifully with our telephone research—everything, that is, except the outcome. Having reached a dead end, we repaired to the place across the street from the movie house, Tony's soul food restaurant/bar. He was too depressed, he said, to order the ribs or anything else, so he settled for a large stein of ale. I ordered a Campari and soda. We sat side by side on ripped red leather barstools, the two sad little piles of notes between us on the bar. I placed Martha's log book on the empty seat next to me.

"No Bruno, no Bruno," Tony repeated from time to time as we slipped deeper into the barroom haze. "Yes, we have no Brunos."

"In fact, we have no nothing," I said. "Not a single mention by any of the ones we reached of Martha's passion—or hobby—or whatever one would call her collecting. Isn't that odd?"

"Why is it odd? She was just there with the clients to deal with their cats. You don't talk about the theater with the guy who comes to wash your venetian blinds, do you?"

"I know, I know. But that doesn't matter in this case. If you have a consuming passion, you manage to make it known. Even to strangers."

"Maybe it has something to do with that Italian word you asked me about. Remember?"

"You mean *aspettando*."

"Yes. And since it means "waiting," maybe everybody is just waiting for Bruno . . . like waiting for Godot."

I grimaced into my drink. Sooner or later Tony always got carried away. And the older he got the less he seemed to be able to control his flights of unreason.

"Well," I said, directing him away from any more fanciful connections, "at least Martha kept excellent records. She was very thorough. And it would have been a lot harder for us to make all those calls if her handwriting had been illegible."

"She wasn't all that good. She wrote down totally wrong numbers for a lot of them."

"Not many," I corrected.

"Fourteen, wasn't it?"

The number, for some reason, intrigued me. Perhaps it was the gloom at the bar. Perhaps it was because I had nothing else to be intrigued by.

"Doesn't that number strike you as strange, Tony?"

"How so?"

"We covered fourteen days in the ledger and it turned out that she made fourteen mistakes about phone numbers."

He found my comment amusing. "What are we getting into here, Swede—numerological mysticism?"

"Let's see how mystical it is." I placed the ledger on top of the bar, opened it, then checked our notes against the pages in Martha's book.

When I finished my examination, I sat upright on the stool, trying to unknot the kinks in my back.

"One mistake for every day, Tony. One and only one wrong number on each day for fourteen consecutive workdays."

"So?"

"So it's obvious. She wrote down one fake

entry each day of the last fourteen days she worked."

"That's a pretty wild conclusion to jump to, isn't it? How do you know they're not just mistakes, that she actually faked them? I mean, she collected a fee on each of those entries. How could they be fakes? Who paid?"

"Fake," I said simply.

"But why? And how come you're so sure?"

"That's what we're going to find out."

"How?"

I flipped the book open to the first "error." The name of the client was John L. Powers and he lived at 241 East 55th Street, in Manhattan. When we called him the operator said the number was not in service. According to Martha's records Mr. Powers's cat was missing and he was afraid it might have fallen from the window of his tenth-floor apartment. But he was too petrified to look.

"Let's pay Mr. Powers a visit, shall we?" I said.

We walked east a few blocks on Houston Street. Then we hailed a cab.

The problem was, number 241 East 55th Street did not exist. Whatever had been on that site was torn down to build a New York Telephone Company switching station. The elderly doorman at the apartment house across the street told us that demolition had occurred years and years ago.

"The next one," Tony said excitedly, nearly

ripping the ledger out of my hands. "Let's see the next one."

The next mistake in Martha's log concerned one Lois Tai. She lived in Chelsea, the book said, on West 19th Street, and her cat had eaten a poisonous houseplant.

There was an apartment building at the address written in Martha's log book, but there was no tenant named Lois Tai. The building super had never heard of her.

We went to a third address, which turned out to be a parking lot.

At address number four, a converted carriage house, the family in residence was just sitting down to milk and cookies. They kept two lovely Irish setters but no cats, and they did not know the person named in Martha's book.

After mistake number six—on Vandam Street—went the way of all the others, we sat down on a stoop and rested. We'd more or less come full circle: we were now back on the fringes of the Village.

"I don't think we have to bother checking any more, do we?" I asked Tony. "Are you convinced now?"

He nodded. "Why would she *do* that?"

"Let's ask her friends."

We walked the few blocks to the VCP office. All the Cat People were in residence, all looking ragged. The phones rang sporadically. Slowly I was beginning to understand their mode of work. All three worked the day shift. Then one worked through until midnight. Then the answering service took over and distributed emergency calls evenly. Either way, no matter the shift, each of the Village Cat People obviously worked a sixty-hour week. I hoped they were making good money. They deserved to.

I asked them for a few minutes of undivided attention. They gave it to me. I told them what Tony and I had found out.

At first their response was silence. Dead silence. Then Ann blurted out: "That's nonsense. That's just plain crazy. Martha was a terribly honest person. Why would she enter false information in the records?"

"And what about the fees?" Libby chimed in. "If she was faking those clients, she still had to account for the fees at the end of the day. That would mean she was paying out of her own pocket. Why would she do a thing like that?"

They began to talk animatedly among themselves, trying out all kinds of theories. I listened patiently. But for the first time I had the feeling that the Village Cat People's suspicions were correct, that Martha Lorenz had been targeted for death, not randomly murdered by an overexcited mugger. Her murder had to do with the distant past. With the vanquished and romantic bohemian era of the Village. With a famous American poet-adventuress. With an empty wooden file box. That probably wasn't all; I

bet the story was even more complex than
all that. But who knew how all those ele-
ments fit together. Perhaps Bruno did, whoever that was.

I looked at my watch. It was nearly five-
thirty. I hadn't called my answering machine in hours. Like most actors and other
societal marginals, I called my machine at
least five times a day. It was a kind of addic-
tion. After all, there could be a job for me
somewhere. There could be a cat-sitting as-
signment. There could be any kind of call.

The only thing I had so far purchased for
the new loft was one of those miraculous
high-tech answering machines. It was no
taller than a paperback mystery novel—and
just as thin. Without any wires whatsoever,
it runs on some kind of computer chip. Not
only can you pull your messages from outside in the wink of an eye but you can in-
struct it that if so and so calls, please
inform her that I am waiting for her at the
north end of the Empire State Building. Of
course, you're able to change your outgoing
message at will, rewind and erase with the
push of a button, leave encoded messages.
That little machine does everything but start
supper for you. It was a mind-blowing piece
of technology and I loved it to death—the
newness hadn't yet worn off.

I called my number while the Village Cat
People were still discoursing. There was only
one message. From Detective Vargas. He left

a number and said there had been a major break in the case.

I hung up and shouted to the crowd, "Please be quiet! The detective on Martha's case has something for us." The silence was immediate.

I dialed Vargas's number. He spoke quietly, clearly, his voice free of emotion. When I hung up, all eyes were upon me. I waited a few beats and then began my short soliloquy:

"I'm afraid all of our efforts now appear to be absurd. The police have announced the arrest of a man in the Lorenz case. He is a habitual offender, currently a resident in a methadone program in my neighborhood. He has confessed to Martha's murder. One of her credit cards was found in his room along with several of the syringes taken from her bag. I am . . . sorry."

Danny Celestino started to say something . . . to protest. But he stopped mid-sentence, out of words. No matter what we had all believed, no matter how strange the bits and pieces of information we had gathered, no matter how intellectually intriguing the chase had become, we all knew that this particular game was over. We all knew we had to walk away now.

8

In the cavernous, very expensive ABC Carpet store, on lower Broadway, an ethereal-looking young salesman was explaining to me the history of a Turkish runner priced at $4,700. As the conversation progressed I realized he expected me to purchase the rug and believed that I was financially capable of doing so. That was nice. I told him I would be back; I had to meet my husband. What a classic prefeminist ploy to escape a salesman. I was a bit ashamed of myself.

An hour later I was in Pierre Deux, on Bleecker Street, inspecting a $7,000 armoire.

All this in the service of furnishing my new dwelling. Of course I was in a fantasy world, but it was fun finding out first what I might do if money were no object. There would be plenty of time for reality.

Alison had accompanied me to Pierre

Deux, but she really wasn't much help because she was still wrapped in a cocoon of joy as a result of her visit to Maud/Piaf. She didn't shut up about that cat . . . going on and on about how beautiful she was and how wonderful the reunion had been and how, spontaneously, the kitty had launched into a few bars of "*Non, Je Ne Regrette Rien.*" Believe me, no one loves hearing cat stories more than yours truly, Alice Nestleton, but my mind was occupied with the furnishing problem. And, I had to admit, that monklike pallet I'd been sleeping on had begun to do its work on my spine.

After two days of make-believe shopping, I decided it was time to get down to basics and buy at least the beginnings of a bed. So I purchased a superfirm mattress at one of those quick delivery places on Sixth Avenue. It arrived late in the afternoon and I was standing in the near-empty loft staring at it there on the floor, sheetless, thinking it was a senior citizen version of something in a hippie commune, when Tony telephoned. Having come into some unexpected money, he was inviting me to dinner at an Italian restaurant. I accepted with pleasure. We met at eight in an old Village restaurant called Mary's, on Bedford Street.

How wonderful it was to taste an old-fashioned antipasto, particularly the olives. Tony was in fine fettle, talking a blue streak about twenty different things, some of which I couldn't follow, none of which I had any real interest in.

Then, suddenly, just before the main course was served, he held up his hands as if to say that he was now ceasing his banter and wished to discuss something important. Politely, I leaned a bit toward him. He looked his handsome, wild best; hair long, face dark and lean, eyes the perennial drama student's—hopeful, frightened, arrogant. I had the sudden urge to reach across the table and touch his face, but I refrained. I'm not sure why. It was a gesture that might have embarrassed me, but not him.

"Listen, Swede, I have been unable to get that whole Martha Lorenz mess out of my mind."

"I figured that, Tony. You seemed very much into it when we were making all those calls."

"Not only was I into it, Swede, but I was beginning to get the chills."

"The chills?"

"Yeah. You know, when you get a part in a play and you know things about the character the moment you read the first line. Almost a mystical convergence of the past and present."

"Calm down, Tony. What in heaven's name is a mystical convergence?"

His voice became lower, more impassioned. "Well, it all began with that stupid word you asked me about."

"*Aspettando*, you mean."

"Right. That started the chills. Funny things were coming into my head. Funny feelings." He paused and tapped a fork on the table.

"Well, I'm waiting, Tony."

"I got the feeling that maybe Martha Lorenz was murdered because she became involved in some ancient Sicilian blood feud. You know, from the old country. Something really evil and vengeful that came across the Atlantic years ago to Greenwich Village. And then resurfaced. Oh, I know it sounds wild. And I know that Martha Lorenz didn't seem the kind of woman who would be involved in such a thing. But I had those chills. And they were deep and cold, Swede."

I sat back and stole a quick glance at the water glass at his right hand. What had he been drinking? I thought he'd had nothing more than a glass of red wine. But he likely had been drinking before he met me. Tony had a weakness for brandy at odd hours of the day. His recitation seemed to reek of alcohol . . . it was too bizarre even for his stage-designer imagination.

He caught me looking at his glass. He knew instantly what I was thinking.

"Damn you, Swede, I'm not drunk. I'm rational and I'm serious."

"Then I'll be rational and serious also, Tony. And blunt, the police have arrested a suspect. The suspect has confessed to the mugging and murder. The suspect was also in possession of some things that belonged to Martha; things she had with her when she rang my bell. Now, it really doesn't matter that all three of the Village Cat People still think she was assassinated in spite of the arrest. And it doesn't matter that you have these mystical chills about the case. And it doesn't matter that I, too, was beginning to think something was fishy. Until the court decides that the confession was obtained under duress or that the objects taken from Martha were planted on the subject . . . until that happens . . . if it ever happens . . . we are out of the case."

He didn't reply. He sat there pouting, staring at his fork until the main dishes arrived. He had veal. I had eggplant. The sudden tension between us didn't hurt our appetites. We cleaned our plates.

Tony ordered brandy with his espresso.

"I forgot to tell you," I said, finally, breaking the silence, "I bought a new mattress—a real one."

"You mean a bed?"

"No, just a mattress."

The coffees were served. I put one cube of sugar in mine and swirled it gently.

"I thought maybe," said I, "you would like to try it out."

He grinned slyly. "That sounds like a pass to me, Swede."

"It's more than a pass, Tony. It's a frank sexual offer."

"Have you ever known me to refuse such an offer?"

"Never."

"I'm going to drink my brandy quickly."

It was an exemplary spring night. We held hands as we walked, like the starstruck young lovers we weren't.

But as we got closer to my new place, we slowed down. It was odd—and maybe peculiarly middle-aged. After all, we had skipped dessert and rushed through the end of our dinner once we'd decided to come home to make love, but as we approached the goal, we slowed down, rather than sped toward it.

It was not that either of us was having second thoughts. Quite the contrary. I enjoyed sex more and more as I got older. So did Tony, it seemed. But what we also had learned to enjoy was the anticipation. In fact, it was now a lovely part of the sex. Much different from when I was younger . . . when sex was all urge and infatuation and shooting stars. I suppose the faster time goes, the more we need to draw it out.

So we talked softly to each other as we took a roundabout tour up Hudson Street, peering in at the mystery bookstore and the antique clothing store, at the gay bars, at the popular new fast-food places like the Cafe Burrito, another example of the un-

fathomable attempt to make the Village over
in the image of a downscale California
beach town.

The streets were teeming with life. While
the East Village had taken over the mantle
of rebellious bohemia, there was no doubt
that the West Village—Greenwich Village—
still was a magnet for all manner of people
looking for all manner of distractions. I
was glad my new place was a bit off the
beaten track for the tourists and rabble-
rousers.

We passed St. Luke's, thought about entering that beautiful church for a spell, decided against it, and turned west toward
Washington Street. Now we were beginning
to pick up our gait. The blocks west of Hudson were usually empty and could even be
a bit threatening. There were many home-
less people in the shadows, the Lower West
Side long perceived by them as a safe
haven.

I opened the heavy street door easily, having become practiced. Tony and I necked se-
riously for a minute or so before heading up
the stairs.

Suddenly he gripped my arm, my left arm,
from behind, so tightly that I cried out. "You
hurt me, you idiot!"

"Shut up! There's someone up there!"

I froze on the stairs, very frightened.

"Were you expecting someone?" he whispered.

"No!"

"Burglars," he said. "Let's go back down and call the police."

Yes, I was frightened. Very frightened. But for some reason I refused. I would be damned if I'd be driven from my own beautiful loft by a bunch of thugs. I wasn't really thinking clearly. I wasn't being brave—I'm not a brave person physically. But I wasn't going to run away right then, not in my home. It never dawned on me that they might have guns or knives.

I shook his hand off and ran up the remaining stairs.

"Come back here!" I heard Tony shout, but then he followed me. We reached my landing together.

I burst out laughing. "Oh, my God, Dr. Leon," I said when I saw my vet standing there. "You scared us half to death."

He smiled at me. Then all I could think was that something was wrong with Bushy or Pancho to bring him here, even though I hadn't called him.

I started to ask him why he was at my door, when, suddenly, Tony stepped in front of me.

I looked past Tony at Dr. Leon again. He was still smiling but he appeared unsteady on his feet. He was leaning against the wall.

Then I saw the great pumping wound in his chest—the blood gushing out in huge spurts.

Tony ripped off his shirt and pressed it against the wound. He and Dr. Leon slid to the floor.

"Go and call for an ambulance, Swede. Fast."

9

Dr. Leon died before the EMS people arrived. He died in Tony's arms, just outside my door. First there had been Martha. Now it was Dr. Leon. The angel of death kept visiting me, wherever I moved.

I went inside, sat down on the new mattress, unable to cry or speak. I just sat there and watched officialdom go through its paces.

One of the officers called Leon's office. His assistant, Peg Oates, rushed over.

A severe-looking man named Detective Crowley interrogated her. She sat at the folding table only five feet from me. Crowley sat opposite her. Bushy was under the table staring at the detective's feet. Pancho was I know not where.

Peg told Crowley that the office was always open late on Wednesdays. Tonight had been no different. She had gone out for dinner. When she returned—around eight-twenty—Dr. Leon was gone. He left a note that the Village Cat People had called him; that Alice Nestleton's cat, Bushy, was having seizures in her new loft; that they were afraid to move him; that he must come. And that is all she knew. She broke down in helpless sobbing soon after Crowley asked his last question and was taken home in a squad car.

When Crowley's colleague arrived a few minutes later, he reported that he'd spoken to all the Village Cat People. Each had denied making any call to Leon's office for any reason. They knew nothing about Bushy's being ill.

Then Crowley interrogated the small, quiet-spoken furniture designer who lived on the first floor. He heard someone ring the street door buzzer about nine—or so he thought. What with the antiquated bell, it was sometimes hard to tell which of the three apartments in the building was being buzzed. At any rate, he was expecting a late delivery and so he buzzed the person in. But then his phone rang. He answered it, conducted a brief conversation, then hung up and went to his door to admit the delivery man who he presumed was waiting.

There was no one at the door. But he heard footsteps on the stairs. He assumed it was a visitor for the new tenant who had inadvertently pushed the wrong bell. No, he had heard no shots. But how could he? He was listening to an opera—*Turandot*.

When Detective Crowley approached me, Tony, being protective of me, fell into step alongside him. Crowley eyed him with suspicion if not outright hostility.

"I'm a good friend of hers," Tony explained. "I came up the stairs with her."

Crowley nodded, as if he understood that completely, then asked: "Are you feeling better?"

"A bit shaky. But yes."

"Are you up to answering some questions?"

I nodded. I kept my eye on the knot of his pastel tie. He was a tall man. He looked a little like Mr. Horne, my high school music teacher.

"Was there anything wrong with your cat?"

"No."

"Did you call Dr. Leon's office for any reason this evening?"

"No."

"Are you familiar with the organization called the Village Cat People?"

"Yes. I have used their services. I know them all."

"None of them were here this evening?"

"No."

"Perhaps earlier?"

"Once. Briefly. But that was more than a week ago."

"Were you friendly with Dr. Leon?"

"Friendly? Well, yes. He was my vet."

"That's not what I mean."

"What do you mean, Detective?"

"Did you have a personal relationship?"

"We were not friends. We were not lovers. I saw him perhaps three times—in his office. That is all."

"Where were you coming from this evening?"

"A restaurant in the neighborhood."

Tony chimed in with the name and street address of the restaurant—and the head waiter's nickname. At this point, Crowley jotted down a couple of notes.

"How long were you in the restaurant?"

"About two hours."

"How long have you been living here?"

"Not very long. Not even two weeks."

"What's your previous address?"

I told him.

"I think I heard someone say you're in television. That right?"

Crowley was beginning to irritate me, which was good, because irritation meant a kind of normalcy. "I am out of work at the moment, actually. But I am an actress, Detective Crowley . . . and a cat-sitter."

Then he looked at Tony, long and hard, as if he were trying to match his face with a mug shot.

Can I see some identification?" he asked.

Tony opened his wallet and gave it to him. The detective removed Tony's driver's license and wrote down the information in his notebook.

"Actually, the only thing I'm wanted for is a set I did at Yale Drama School in 1981." The quip went over Crowley's head.

Then the detective flipped his notebook closed.

"Was it robbery?" Tony asked.

"No. Nothing was taken. The man had a wallet full of credit cards and three hundred dollars in cash—untouched."

"So there was someone up here waiting for him?" I asked.

"Could be. But I tend to doubt it. Doesn't look like there was a struggle. No sign that Leon tried to run. He was shot right outside your door in the chest at point-blank range. I figure the vet and his killer might just have come into the building together. Went up the stairs together. He never expected it."

"You mean they came as friends?" Tony asked. "Maybe at the end of a friendship?"

"I mean," Crowley said harshly, "one didn't expect the other to shoot him."

At long last, Crowley left us. The loft remained a jumble of noise for another hour or so. Then, as suddenly as the horror had exploded, it vanished.

All was quiet. I sat on the mattress. Tony was on a folding chair. He had turned off the main loft light that consisted only of a cluster of three bulbs in the ceiling, controlled by a wall switch. I needed lamps, too.

Moonlight flooded the room. Bushy was on one window ledge, staring west. Pancho lay on his back on another ledge, his paws up in the air, as if he were inspecting them for calluses.

"Do you want me to make you some tea?" Tony asked kindly.

"I don't want any tea."

"You want me to go out and get some aspirin?"

"I have aspirin."

He was shifting around on the chair, uncomfortable in the shirt I had given him to replace the one he had ripped off to stanch Dr. Leon's bleeding. The green-checked flannel shirt, tight and constricting, was actually an old one of his. He'd left it at my flat years ago. Tony still looked like a boy in many respects, but he had put on considerable weight. I chalked it up to alcohol, and wondered what another twenty-five pounds would look like around my own midriff.

"What do we do now, Swede?" he suddenly asked pathetically.

"Concerning what?"

"You know what I'm talking about."

"Yes, I do. I surely do. And I don't know what to do."

"What's going on, Swede?"

"A whole lot of death, Tony." Then I hoisted myself up and began to walk around the place gingerly, tentatively, as if I were recovering from a fall.

My pace quickened steadily until I was virtually trotting, doing laps around the room. And then, obviously in the throes of a one-minute nervous breakdown, I began to dance.

"What the hell are you doing?" I heard Tony call out, fear in his voice.

I remember screaming at him: "Why do you ask me what we're going to do? Why don't you ask what Martha Lorenz and Dr. Leon are going to do?"

"But they're dead."

I nodded my head wearily. And then I began to cry. I was convinced I would never stop.

Then I remember nothing.

It was about three in the morning when I awoke. Tony was next to me on the mattress, fully dressed. And Bushy was a foot away, on the floor, staring at me pensively. I could see Pancho on one of the chairs.

"Better?" Tony asked.

"Your shirt looks very silly," I said. I loosened it for him. He gave me a very tender kiss, and before I knew it, we were making love.

"I'd like a glass of water," I said.

He left the bed and returned with a tall, cool drink. I drank it in one gulp.

"You know, Tony, that detective is going to have our phone checked—to see if we made the call to Dr. Leon."

"What do you have to worry about? You didn't make the call. I assume he'll check the Village Cat People phone, too. And Leon's phone. It's just procedure."

I put the glass down on the floor.

"Do you remember what I said to you in the restaurant, Tony?"

"About the Martha Lorenz murder?"

"Yes. Well, I retract everything I said. Every bloody word."

Pancho and Bushy, in a rare synchronized move, scooted close to us.

"In fact, Tony, I don't really care how many suspects Detective Vargas arrests in the Martha Lorenz murder or what kind of evidence he has. And I don't give a damn what this Detective Crowley finds. Because now you and I know something that they simply don't know or don't understand— that these two deaths were connected. And that two people died somehow, in some way, from—" I stopped. I couldn't articulate it.

"From what?" Tony pressed.

"I don't know. But it is closer to your wild theory than we thought. You know . . . those chills you got. Well, now I have them. Something went wrong in Greenwich Village. Yes, isn't that crazy, Tony? But that's what I think. Something about the Village, a long time ago. Something that was on the walls of Martha's apartment and in her card file. Something about Bruno, whoever he is. Something about Edna Saint Vincent Millay. Something very crazy and complex. Something that would make sane people murder."

"I'm with you, Swede."

"Good. So the first thing I'll do in the morning is pay a visit to Dr. Leon's assistant."

"Peg Oates?"

"Correct. There was something about that woman. I don't know what . . . just something. I didn't like her, Tony."

I handed him the empty glass so he could bring me a refill.

10

I stared at the gold-plated sign just to the left of the door. AMOS LEON, DVM, it read. On a normal day the waiting room would be crazy with the sounds of chirping and yipping and whining. But of course this wasn't a normal day. I rang the little illuminated doorbell.

No, everything was changed now. Dr. Leon was dead—murdered—the second corpse to be left at my door. Everything that Alice Nestleton touched was now problematic, so I hesitated before grasping the doorknob. I was frightened of the object, I realized. I had become frightened of doorknobs. Please, Dr. Freud, give me some solace.

I turned the knob finally, forcefully, and walked inside. I waited in the small cubicle that was scanned by a television camera from the interior office. Then I was buzzed through the second door.

There was not a single cat, dog, canary, turtle, or hamster in sight. There was only Peg Oates seated at the large reception desk. She was just finishing up a phone conversation. I saw Dr. Leon's appointment book opened to today's date. On the floor next to her desk were a few flattened cartons tied together with twine. Peg looked up at me with tired, tired eyes.

She was the kind of woman who seemed to have been born at the age of thirty-seven. She was terribly thin with dullish blond hair, and very well dressed except for the godawful costume jewelry she seemed to be so fond of. Yet she somehow appeared to know how awful it was, and wanted you to know she knew. Peg had always been solicitous and gentle enough with the animals, but there was something eternally grim in her manner. As though she expected the worst to happen at the earliest possible moment. I had met her many times before in various incarnations; head of a typing pool, wardrobe mistress, restaurant manager. She always had a particular passion: sometimes it was music; sometimes it was food; sometimes it was hiking; but it was rarely people.

"What are you doing here, Miss Nestleton?" she asked.

"I just want to ask you a few questions."

"The practice is out of business."

"I mean about Dr. Leon."

"Dr. Leon is dead. What difference would any questions make?"

"I mean about his murder, Miss Oates."

"People call me Peg. And when did you join the police department?"

"You do understand that Dr. Leon was found murdered right in front of my apartment?"

"I don't have amnesia."

I recalled what I'd said to Tony about Peg Oates, and was certain now that I'd been right to feel uneasy about her. This woman hated me. And I hadn't the slightest idea why.

"Did he ever sleep in this office when he worked late?" I asked.

No answer.

"Was Dr. Leon ever married?"

She turned her back to me and busied herself with cutting the string from the cartons.

"Was he gay?"

No answer.

"If not gay, did he have a current woman friend . . . a mistress?"

Peg looked at me defiantly but still did not speak. But this time I had the distinct impression that she wanted to say something and was holding back. It occurred to me that my perception that she hated me might be all wet. She could simply be a woman lost in grief over the death of her boss, friend, confidant. Of course! There was every possibility that she and Leon had been lovers.

But she staunchly refused to talk.

"Did he ever collect memorabilia about Greenwich Village?" I pressed.

She put the scissors down then and folded her hands neatly. "Do you know the story of Alexander the Great and the Cynic philosopher Diogenes?"

I was startled by her question. I tried to remember if I knew such a story. Nope.

"I'm sorry I don't," I admitted, "but to be honest I don't really see what that has to do with anything."

She ignored my remark and told me this story: "The Great Alexander sought out Diogenes for wisdom. He found the philosopher resting in his usual place—a bathtub in the marketplace. Alexander rushed over to him and offered to grant him any wish if only he would impart his precious wisdom to the Conqueror of the Known World. Diogenes told him to bend over because he wanted to whisper in his ear. The Great Alexander bent over the tub, waiting. Diogenes whispered: 'Get out of my light.' "

I knew it was time to go.

Back in my loft, I paced in front of Tony and Alison. I was in a foul mood.

"I assume the interview didn't go well," Tony said.

"You assume correctly. And if I was stupid

enough to start dealing with these murders
by interviews . . . then I deserve what I got."

"Well, why not interviews? We ain't got
much. We might as well start with living,
breathing witnesses."

"Not witnesses, Tony. There are no witnesses. All we have are tenuous connections. Two murders that we think are
connected. One of the victims collected bohemian memorabilia, knew someone named
Bruno, and made fake entries in her log
book. The other we know nothing about except that he dealt with the other victim professionally. The Village Cat People and Dr.
Leon were inextricably linked. Each used
the other as a reference, as a resource."

"There's another connection," Alison said
brightly.

"What?"

"They were both killed at your doorstep."

"Right you are . . . and that's why I'm
going to clean up the blood."

We all sat down at the folding table.
Bushy joined us, taking what had become
his usual place on Alison's lap. Sometimes
he looked as if he wanted to take notes.

"I think now we should proceed methodically. Tony and I will go back to the Cat People office and look over the other log books.
Maybe we can find this mysterious Bruno
through them. Maybe one of the Cat People
switched assignments once with Martha

and forgot about it. We'll do just what we did with Martha's log . . . make phone calls."

Tony nodded happily. He seemed to love making phone calls.

"And what do I do?" Alison asked.

"I'd like you to visit every store in the area that sells the kind of thing Martha was interested in—secondhand shops, antique stores, poster shops, bookstores—whatever you can think of, I want to know if Martha was a regular at any of them. If she collected with a certain emphasis. Did she really love old photos or menus or what? What was her priority? And was it only for the golden age of Village bohemia . . . circa 1919? Or were there other eras? Did she come in alone? If not, get a description of her companions. And ask specifically about Dr. Leon. Do any of the shopkeepers know him or know of him? We have to tie Dr. Leon and Martha together."

Alison left first. Tony and I dawdled. We had lunch together in the Lost Diner. Then we meandered to the Village Cat People office on Morton Street. For some reason we kept hesitating before entering even though we were anxious to get to work . . . anxious to get on it. It was, like everything in this case, contradictory and inexplicable.

But once inside the office we realized we had done well to meander. They were not happy to see us.

"I thought you told us it was futile to continue the investigation because the police have arrested Martha's murderer," Ann said a bit defiantly.

"But that was before Dr. Leon was murdered."

"What does one have to do with the other?" asked Libby.

"I don't know yet, but it's enough to start looking some more."

"For bogus entries in logs?" Danny asked contemptuously.

"For starters, yes," I said.

Libby turned suddenly and slammed a notepad she was holding onto the top of one of the crowded desks with such a fury that it sounded like a gun shot. I nearly jumped out of my skin.

"What is the matter with you?" Ann asked, angry at the crazy eruption.

"I'm sorry. Damn. I'm sorry. I was just thinking how I'm going to miss Dr. Leon. I'm tired of losing friends."

"Everybody is going to miss him," Ann choked out. She turned away quickly.

Danny kept shaking his head sadly. "Well, we have a lot of good memories," he said.

"Yes, they are . . . Yes, they are good," Ann affirmed through her tears.

"Remember his dream? His messianic fantasy?" Libby asked.

What were they talking about? I wanted to hear this.

"You mean his land and machine dream?" Danny said.

They all laughed through tears at their shared memory.

"What was Dr. Leon's dream?" I asked.

Libby was glad to tell me. "He needed twenty million dollars, he told us. Then he was going to buy one hundred acres of prime Hudson River frontage in upstate New York and he was going to turn the entire place into a state-of-the-art animal hospice. No fees charged. No questions asked. Just bring in the sick and wounded. But that was only part of it. Attached to the hospice was going to be a fleet of EMS emergency vehicles, outfitted only for animals, and they were going to cruise the big city day and night and rescue any animals in trouble and bring them up to the hospice. It was just like him to have a fantasy like that."

Her retelling of Dr. Leon's dream made them all morose and no further words were said. They went back to doing their work: manning phones; dispensing advice; going out on house calls. Tony and I appropriated a couple of phones and started making the same calls again: did they know someone named Bruno; had they ever met Martha; did they collect Village memorabilia or know anyone who did. Most of the queries turned up nothing, of course, because these were not Martha's logs, but they had to be gone through. We worked late into the afternoon, then went out to eat. When we came back the Cat People were gone and the answering service was picking up all the calls.

Basillio and I started our calls again. "It's almost seven now, Tony; we'll work until ten and then call it a night. Okay?" He nodded and dialed.

It was about forty-five minutes later that Tony found something. At first all he said was: "You want to know something funny, Swede?" But I was on the phone and I didn't. Then about ten minutes later, he said: "I take it back. It isn't funny."

"What are you talking about, Tony?"

He grinned his grin and slid one of the ledgers over my notes. "Take a peep."

"What am I looking at?"

"A genuine one hundred percent bogus entry."

"Like Martha's?"

"Exactly," he affirmed, tapping the ledger paper with his finger. "I've turned up one phony number after another. And it's even better than that. These bogus entries are on the same days and at the same time as Martha's."

"Are you sure?"

"Absolutely. Same days. Same times. Same kind of fake name and phone number. Same kind of fake fee received."

"Whose ledger is it?"

"Danny Celestino's."

"I see." I didn't speak for a long time after

that. When I finally did, it was merely to ask Tony: "How about going for a long walk with me?"

"Now?"

"Right now."

11

"Are you sure, Tony? Are you absolutely sure?" I kept asking as we walked. We had turned into West Broadway and were going south into Tribeca. It didn't matter where we went, really. All I wanted to do was shake the cobwebs out of my head, and make sense out of what he had discovered. It was, I knew, a breakthrough.

"Of course I'm sure. Celestino's book entries are as fake as Martha's. Phony numbers. Same days. Same times."

"And you didn't find any fake entries in the other ledgers—Libby's or Ann's?"

"I didn't find any."

"Well, neither did I."

"Hey—slow down, will you, Swede? I can never keep up with you when you go into that shit-kicking dairy farmer's gait."

Tony was right. Whenever I got agitated I slipped into my grandmother's mode of walking. It meant simply taking very long strides. One learned to do that on a dairy farm because there was either mud or muck or slush all year long. And therefore one had to wear boots all the time. And boots were heavy. And they were heavier pulling them out of muck. So you had to take long strides simply because that would lessen the amount of "setting 'em down and pulling 'em up."

I slowed down. We crossed Canal Street, into Tribeca. Then I slipped my arm into his and said: "You know, Tony, I think maybe we have been all kinds of fools."

"How so?"

"Coming up with grand conspiracy theories . . . chills . . . you know, the whole works."

"What I found out changes everything?"

"It sure does. It changes, reveals, turns upside down. Mr. Celestino's fake entries are like a glass of lemonade—simple, uncomplicated."

We had walked into the heart of Tribeca.

"Speaking of lemonade . . ." Tony said and then pointed to a bar on the corner called Walkers.

We walked inside. My agitation was gone. I was smiling, almost beatific. The stupid thing had become clear. It was the most banal of scenarios.

Tony ordered a brandy, soda on the side. I ordered a Lillet.

"Do you know where Celestino lives?" I asked Tony.

"Yes. His address and phone number was on the ledger. On Sixth Street, just east of Second."

"Let's go there now!"

"Are you serious?"

"Quite serious. What's the matter, Tony? Don't you like the young man? He is the spitting image of you, twenty years ago."

"I resent that."

"And I think he got into the same kind of trouble that you would get into in those years."

"Like what?"

"Like a *ménage à trois*."

"You've lost me."

"Only this one ended up in murder. Finish your drink, Basillio. Let's pay him a visit. I'll explain it to both of you at the same time."

"You always hold back, don't you, Swede?"

I glared at him. Something about his statement was mighty unfriendly.

"You used to be able to drink a lot of brandy without getting ugly, Tony."

He raised his hands in apology.

"You don't have to come with me, Tony. I can handle this alone. I'm appreciative of what you found out because it changes everything. But you don't have to continue. Understand?"

"Calm down, Swede. I'm with you in this to the end."

"Good. Because I think the end is near. It was always near. Just too large to see."

Danny lived on the first floor of an old-fashioned Lower East Side tenement. No working locks. No working bells.

He grimaced when he opened the door and saw us.

"I don't think he expected us, Tony," I said humorously.

But Danny didn't find that humorous. "It's a bit late," he said coldly.

"We won't stay more than a minute," I assured him. "Just wanted to clear up a few things."

"Concerning what?"

"Concerning why you murdered Dr. Leon."

He looked at me blankly. Then he looked at Tony. "Has your friend flipped or something?"

Tony shrugged.

Meanwhile, I walked into the apartment, which was more like an overboard set decorator's idea of a tenement apartment than a real apartment. No down-at-the-heels detail had been overlooked: bathtub in the kitchen, splintered window sashes, sagging ceiling, rusting fire escape.

"You see," I said calmly, "we know about the bogus entries in your log book."

"So what?" he asked aggressively, leaving the apartment door ajar.

"Your phony entries coincide with Martha's phony ones, Danny. The same days, the same times, the same lies."

"So what?" he repeated threateningly.

"Well, here's what I think, Danny. I think you and Martha falsified those entries so you could sneak off to make love some-where—here or her place, or maybe even a hotel. Now, I ask myself: Why all the decep-tion? You were both free, unmarried adults. And the answer is, because Martha proba-bly had another lover who wouldn't take kindly to it. And that man was Dr. Leon. Then, tragedy strikes. Martha is killed by an addict, a street criminal. You become de-ranged. Probably because you and she planned to leave the Village Cat People— maybe even leave the city. But Martha wasn't ready to do it yet. She wouldn't break off with Dr. Leon. Perhaps he even had some terrible hold on her and she *couldn't* have broken it off with him. In any case you blame him for her death. You baited a trap for him—called him and said there was an emergency at my place. And when he showed up there you killed him."

Danny continued to stare at me after I fin-ished my summation. He didn't say a word. But he sat down on a ratty sofa and buried his face in his hands.

When he looked up, finally, he said, "Jesus! You are one crazy lady." And he began to laugh. Hugely. Deep belly laughs.

His response angered Basillio, who approached him menacingly. "You think the murder of that girl is funny, do you?" he said to the young man.

"You're both nuts, you know that?" Danny shouted suddenly. "What do you think this is—some old potboiler of a movie or something? Sure I faked those entries. And so did Marty. And, yes, we were together at those times. But we weren't in some stupid hotel *shtupping* behind anybody's back. We were just taking cat food and supplies to the Foundation."

"The what?" I asked. "What foundation?"

"We had to fake the books because we didn't know if Libby and Ann would appreciate us taking Cat People supplies to the Foundation—giving stuff away. Oh, we expected to be able to make up for it, pay for the stuff someday. But the only crime I committed . . . we committed . . . was shorting the company a few bucks a month. And that sure as hell ain't murder."

"You didn't answer me. What foundation are you talking about?"

"I can't explain it to you. But I'll show it to you."

"Don't talk in riddles, Danny."

"I'm not talking in anything. I can't explain it, I'm telling you. Just meet me tomorrow morning on the corner of Carmine and Bleecker. Nine o'clock. And I'll show you the Foundation."

We'd reached a standoff. I was defeated and confused. And it must have shown.

Danny mocked me. "What's wrong, Miss Marple? Afraid the killer's going to skip town? Why don't you handcuff me to the bed? . . . Oh, that's right . . . I don't have one. Handcuff me to the sofa till nine tomorrow morning."

"What do you want to do, Swede?" Tony said.

What could I do? I surely couldn't arrest him. I had no power, no proof, no right even to be in the young man's home. "All right. Tomorrow then," I said.

Tony and I cabbed across town to my place. Alison was in the apartment, waiting for me, paper coffee cup in hand. "What is it, Aunt Alice? You don't look well."

"She's . . . tired, Alison. Real tired," Tony said, easing me onto a folding chair.

"I just wanted to tell you what I found out," she said apologetically. "It won't take long."

I nodded. Tony tried holding my hand but I pushed him away. I didn't want compassion just then. I wanted comprehension.

"Several store owners recognized Martha Lorenz from the photo I showed them," she reported. "They said she was an inveterate browser. She was always on the lookout for items relating to Edna Saint Vincent Millay when she incarnated the bohemian ideal and half the men in the Village were in love with her. But nothing Martha ever bought, according to the shopkeepers, was worth much of anything."

"Go on."

"Well, there isn't much more. But," she said with a self-satisfied smile, "we know what that last bit of information means now, don't we?"

"No, Alison, I'm not sure we do. What?"

"It means that whoever so fastidiously looted Martha's apartment of all her treasures didn't take the items for their monetary value."

"Yes, of course you're right. Good thinking, Alison."

I was sorry if my response sounded lackluster. There didn't seem a lot more for me to say. I got up to feed the cats.

Should we have believed Celestino? Was there really such a thing as the "Foundation"? Would he really show up tomorrow at Carmine and Bleecker streets? I looked over worriedly at Basillio.

Tony waved his hand, as if to say everything would be all right. As if he knew everything I was thinking.

12

We were early. Tony and I stood waiting in front of the weathered church at the corner Danny had described. We'd already begun to worry that he'd stand us up, that we'd been had.

But at five past nine he arrived. He appeared nervous, agitated. He didn't greet us and never broke his stride; he only motioned with his head that we were to follow him.

We walked north on Bleecker for about half a block. Then, Tony and I dogging the young man's steps, we turned into . . . a bakery!

Tony shot me a look.

I shook my head. "Don't ask, Tony. I'm as much in the dark as you are."

Once inside the store, Danny didn't stop at the counter. He didn't even speak to the man in the white apron who was busily bagging the warmly fragrant loaves of white and whole-wheat breads. Instead, we were marched straight through the room and out the back, through a long hallway and a bolted door to which Danny had the key. When we emerged into the daylight again, we were in a backyard.

But it was like no Village yard I'd ever been in before. A high wire mesh fence separated it from the adjacent properties and, high above us, the wire mesh closed over—encasing the entire yard and us in it.

We weren't the only ones inside the wire cage. There must have been fifty cats there—lolling about on plastic chairs, sleeping peacefully in the sun, breakfasting, frolicking. They all seemed quite content. But they were not your normal felines. Several appeared to be hard-pressed strays. Many were obviously wounded or crippled. The lame, the halt, and the blind were in residence.

An old woman sat wordlessly in a wheelchair near the mesh fence. I surmised that she was paralyzed. She was wrapped in several blankets even though the morning air was fresh and warm.

A second woman was methodically setting out dishes of cat food. She looked even older than the one in the wheelchair. Her skeleton was there for all to see beneath her skin. Yet she moved with a determined power, like a strong, starved hawk.

118   *Lydia Adamson*

"That's Claire Agoste," Danny whispered to me. "The one in the wheelchair is Simone Ray. They're both over ninety."

As she fed the cats, Claire talked a blue streak of nonsense. But the kits seemed to be listening.

"Why is this called a foundation?" I managed to ask in spite of the shock of finding myself in this strange world.

" 'Cause it started with money given to Claire by a man in the late 1920s. He was a cat-loving, crazy old guy called Bruno who used to wander around the Village reciting his poetry with a cat on his shoulder."

"And you said nothing," I retorted bitterly, "when that name showed up in Martha's card file and I asked everyone who Bruno could possibly be? You let me waste all that—"

"I know, I know. You must understand. Martha and I didn't want the others to find out we were helping the old ladies during our working hours."

"Uh oh, here she comes," I heard Tony warn us under his breath.

And Claire Agoste *was* coming, walking with a purposeful stride. She took me by the arm as if she had known me for years and started to introduce me to all her charges. Her grip was strong. She spoke quickly, her speech a bit slurred. And once she introduced me to a particular cat and began to relate the circumstances under which it had come to live at the Foundation, her voice became clear and the words easily understood.

"So this one was hit by a motorbike on Perry Street. Can you imagine it? But now she's fine. She's a fine, strong pussy cat—aren't you, Della? Even if she cannot move so fast now, she helps me keep track of all the others. . . . What is your name, young woman? I keep forgetting it."

"I'm Alice Nestleton," I said as we moved on to the next resident. For the first time, I noticed there were several kittens in the backyard. Three of them were playing tug-of-war with the bottom of Simone Ray's wheelchair blanket.

"You must be one of Danny's friends," she said suddenly, as if that explained it all. She stopped, seemed to be thinking, then said, "I like your Danny very much except for that vein on the side of his head. Do you see it? Popping and sticking out and pumping. I say . . . never trust a young man with a prominent vein."

We started to walk on, then Claire stopped. "You must know Martha?" she asked.

"Yes," I said, "I do." I was beginning to feel a great affection for this ancient lady.

"I mean, I *knew* Martha," I said again, this time consciously changing the verb to the past tense.

"And this is Horatio," she said, bending

down next to a very large, very badly scarred red tabby. "Some bad boys got hold of him. But he is going to be fine. Aren't you, my Horatio? Aren't you?"

The big old thing purred and tried to turn over to offer his belly for a scratch, but he couldn't quite make it. I must have gasped with the effort to fight back the tears in my eyes.

"Trust me," Claire said to me firmly, "Horatio will be fine."

"I trust you."

"Good. Now, you must remember to tell Martha that I need Bruno's poems back. I should not have let her take them. But, you know, she loves Bruno's poems so. They are so pretty."

So she didn't know what had happened to Martha. I didn't know what to say. I looked to Danny for help, but he was explaining something to Tony over on the far side of the yard. I saw him pointing up the fencing.

"Poems? What poems are those, Mrs. Agoste?"

"Bruno's poems!" she said emphatically, as if repeating it should be explanation enough. "Martha took about twenty of them. The paper was falling apart. Even his best one—'Madonna at the Barf'—even that one was falling apart. So she told me she would get them recopied nicely and I could have as many copies as I wanted. She was going to use one of those computers. Very smart of

Martha. She is a smart girl, no doubt of that. But tell her to please given them back. I must have those poems back."

Had these "poems" been part of the Bruno file in Martha's apartment? Had to be. Had to be.

I turned the old lady then. "Look. Mrs. Agoste. I feel I must tell you. Well . . . you should know that Martha . . . is dead."

She looked at me harshly, then smiled, then patted my face gently. "Yes, yes. But tell her I need the poems back. They are all that's left of poor Bruno. I don't even know where his ashes are."

She pulled me along. "Come. Say hello to Bella, the one-eyed beauty."

Soon we were approaching a beautiful but quite small burnished-coat cat—largely Siamese—who was sitting quietly near a bowl of water, watching it speculatively. Claire scooped up little Bella in her arms. "I brush her often. Look at her coat. She how it shines?"

I nodded appreciatively.

"Oh, I love this Bella," the old woman said. "I love this Bella so much!" Claire looked at me fiercely. "Do you know why I love her?"

It was the kind of question that demanded an answer. But I could only think of the obvious, so I said nothing.

"Ah, I will tell you why," she said acidly. Then she held the cat away from her chest and gazed proudly upon her. "Look at her. Bella," she pronounced proudly, "has no master. No law. No god. That means she can be trusted. Unlike humans."

It was a puzzling statement. Such a sudden philosophical turn of phrase from the lips of the old lady, that I was quite dazed.

"Do you hear me?" she thundered. "No masters! No laws! No gods!" Then she kissed Bella and released her.

Claire walked off to continue her tasks alone. I went over to join Danny and Basillio. I told them what the old woman had said. Danny only shrugged. "She's old—very old. She says lots of strange things. She doesn't even accept the fact that Marty is gone . . . dead, I mean."

"Did Dr. Leon help out here, too?" I asked, remembering Libby's description of the veterinarian's fantasy—that high-tech animal hospice.

"I don't know. Maybe. Probably. A lot of people help them with money and time."

Tony and I left the Foundation a half hour later. Danny stayed behind to help with the feeding.

We walked slowly back to my apartment. I was silent, and could feel myself slipping into a depression. Once again my inspired analysis of events—in this case the faked entries in Danny's and Martha's log books—had turned out to be nonsense.

Tony wanted to come upstairs with me. I

said I wanted to be alone. He stomped off angrily. There was nothing I could do.

Once inside, I sat forlornly in the empty apartment. The sunlight was tumbling through all the windows. Pancho and Bushy seemed happy, in their fashion. It was nowhere near suppertime. They didn't need me.

The depression was coming in larger waves now . . . washing over me. I had to do something. The windows, I thought. Clean those giant windows.

Yes, that was the ticket. My windows were the old-fashioned industrial type, with steel fittings. They must be accumulating an enormous amount of dust. I'll get a damp cloth and go over every piece of iron on every window frame, I said to myself in my possessed state. Like one of those dizzy women in the old TV ads, scrubbing away in their high heels and cultured pearls, I would clean my way out of this depression.

I set to work furiously. I held one rag under running water, squeezed it out, did the window, then went back to the sink to start the process all over again. It was a singularly inefficient way to get the job done—ludicrous, in fact, and exhausting. Which was exactly the way I wanted it. The two cats watched me with alternating pity and absolute ennui.

It took two hours to complete the job. Then I decided to wax the floors. I felt I could keep the depression at bay only if I kept working at top speed. The floors took another two hours.

Then I dusted the pathetic bridge table and all four of the folding chairs.

Then took a wire brush to the bathroom.

Then took a boar's hair brush to the cats.

I was ravenous. I heated a can of Progresso lentil soup. After I'd eaten I turned the mattress over. It was almost seven P.M. I lay down to think about my next move.

And that was the last thing I remember before the ringing of the phone wrenched me out of a deep sleep.

The clock read thirty-five minutes past midnight. I was dazed from the deepness of the sleep. Who could be calling me at this hour?

At first the voice was unfamiliar. "Alice Nestleton," it said, "you will never guess where I am." Then the haze lifted. It was Tony. He had been drinking. I was suddenly furious at my overgrown, overaged adolescent.

"I'm at Walkers, honey. You know, the bar we were in together the other day."

"Tony, it's past midnight. You just woke me from a sound sleep. What are you up to?"

"Enlightenment, Swede."

"Spelled B-R-A-N-D-Y."

"You think so, huh? Well, I have some news for you that will stupefy you."

"I am already stupefied, thank you."

"No. Listen. Something has been bothering me all day. About what that old woman said to you. You know . . . you told me and Danny the old bat said she loved cats because they have no laws, no gods, and . . . what else? . . . oh, yeah, no masters. 'They can be trusted.' That's what she said—right?—not like people."

"That's exactly what she said."

"Yes, well, it's been eating me all day and all night. So finally I end up here in uh . . . what do they call this place . . . Walkers. And that's where it came to me. About twenty minutes ago. While they were playing that Otis Redding song I like. The one about the docks. What's the name of that song?"

"*What* came to you, Tony?"

"It's a slogan."

"What's a slogan?"

" 'No gods, no laws, no masters.' It was one of the most popular slogans of the Italian Anarchist Movement in the U.S. in the early part of this century."

I sat up. All I knew about the Italian anarchists was what I had read in my high school history book. They were a small band of fanatics and terrorists who went around bombing things and assassinating kings, politicians, financiers, and god knows who else.

"Tony, do you think it's possible that

Bruno the bohemian poet was an Anarchist?"

"Sure it's possible. The anarchists were often poets, and they had close ties to the surrealists."

My mind was beginning to race. It was as if Tony had just knocked down a wall.

"Wait, Swede, there's more. When I was in college I did a paper on the Sacco-Vanzetti case for a political science course. It was a good paper. I got an A."

"Sacco and Vanzetti were anarchists, weren't they?"

"Yes. Well, one definitely and the other an anarchist sympathizer. But the important thing is that after the executions in 1927, there were many so-called reprisals against the government and prosecutors. Bombings, break-ins, robberies. And they painted graffiti on public buildings everywhere—a kind of warning." He paused and then said playfully into the phone: "Guess what one of those warnings said."

"I haven't the slightest idea."

"It said 'Awaiting the hour of vengeance.' Or, in Italian, '*Aspettando l'ora di vendetta.*' "

"You're not making this up, are you, Tony?"

"I'm not making it up. It's all true."

"If Bruno was an anarchist as well as a poet, then it's possible that the money he gave to the Foundation back then was gotten by theft. Am I right?"

"You're damn straight. At least, it's a very strong possibility. They robbed for two reasons, if I remember. Like the IRA and the Basque nationalists, for example, they robbed to support their organization. But they also committed crimes for aesthetic reasons. They liked to loot the homes of rich people because they couldn't stand the fact that the rich could buy treasures . . . artwork."

There was a pause. Dimly, I heard another voice on the wire; someone was talking to Tony. The bartender? Probably. Then Tony spoke into the receiver again. "Sorry, Swede. I was just persuaded into a refill. Now, where was I? Oh, right. You know, the anarchists had a very serious philosophy. The press made them out to be fools and terrorists and beneath contempt. But it was a strong movement then. They weren't all Italian groups either. There were Jewish anarchists, too, and Irish anarchists and WASP anarchists. And there were close ties between the anarchists and the International Workers of the World—the Wobblies. But they splintered the left in this country because they hated the communists and the socialists, and were in turn hated by them. The papers did have one thing right, though: those guys could be deadly. You know this World Trade Center bombing recently? By Islamic fundamentalists. Well, in 1920 the anarchists bombed the House of

Morgan banking firm in the Wall Street area. It was much worse than the Trade Center thing. More than forty people were killed back then, and thousands injured. To this day, it remains the worst terrorist attack ever committed in this city."

"Tony, slow down! You're talking too quickly."

"Oh, sorry. I'm just excited."

I was excited, too. For the first time I could see the beginnings of the forest and not just weird individual trees. The contours were of Martha Lorenz's obsessions: with the bohemian heartthrob poet, Edna St. Vincent Millay. With the eccentric, cat-loving poet named Bruno, aka Bruno the Anarchist. With the Foundation. With a time and a place many years ago. And with Bruno's poems—particularly the one called "Madonna at the Bar."

"Tony," I said, "stay where you are. I'm going to grab a taxi. I'll be down there in ten minutes."

"That's the best news I've heard all day, Swede. The only thing I like better than sleeping with you is drinking with you."

"We're not going to be drinking, Tony."

"Oh."

"Sorry to disappoint you but we're going elsewhere."

"Where?"

"About the year 1924."

I didn't wait for a response. I hung up and

dressed myself as quickly as I could, all in black, from head to toe. Alice Nestleton— aging bohemian wraith.

The cab driver waited while I collected Tony, then dropped us at Hudson and Barrow. The moment we stepped out, Tony inhaled deeply. "The magic didn't work, Swede. I don't think we made it back to the twenties. It still feels like the nineteen nineties to me."

The night was clear and mild. The streets were empty. It was one o'clock in the morning. We walked slowly east on Barrow, crossed over to Bedford, and then turned south. But not far. I halted in front of Number 86 Bedford Street.

"What's this?" Tony asked.

"Open the door."

"What do you mean—just walk in on the people who live here?"

"Just push the door open, Tony."

He did. And we were suddenly in a small, gloomily lighted restaurant. It was pretty late for dinner; not a soul was seated at any of the ancient wooden booths. We walked farther in, to the bar area. Bar space was at a premium—it was a tiny affair with high wood stools. A crowd of college students sat drinking beer, starting spring break early, I guessed.

"Are you buying?" Tony asked me cheerily.

I placed my hands firmly in the small of

his back and moved him along. We exited
the bar area through a nearby door and
found ourselves in a small, bare courtyard.
A few steps and we were back out on the
street again—this time on Barrow Street.

"It's kind of like a ride at the carnival,
isn't it? In one door and out the other. Want
to do it again, Tony?"

"What the hell was that all about?" Tony
asked as I led him in a circle, back around
to the Bedford Street entrance.

"That, dear Tony, was Chumley's."

"Oh, right! That's a famous old bar, isn't
it? Used to be a speakeasy, the story goes."

"Yes. And did you see her at the bar?"

"Who?"

"The madonna, of course."

"Madonna was at that bar?"

"Not her, Tony. I mean *the* madonna—
'Madonna at the Bar.' Edna Saint Vincent
Millay." I pressed on before he could an-
swer: "And did you see the crush of bohemi-
ans? Writers and poets and radicals of all
sorts. Did you get a look at them, Tony?
And the actors and actresses from the
Provincetown Playhouse on MacDougal.
They were there, too."

"I think you'd better get hold of yourself,
Swede. I know damn well what I saw. And it
wasn't what you just described."

"Of course not, Tony. I was just setting
the *mise en scene.*"

I took his hand and we walked one block south on Bedford Street. "Look at that, Tony," I said, pointing to a tiny, dilapidated, boarded-up house.

"I'm looking."

"That, Basillio, is 75½ Bedford. The last place in the Village that Edna lived. You know, Tony, the first time I came to the Village, I walked over here to see her little house. Almost as if it were a shrine. Because she meant a lot to me when I was young."

"It's really run down."

"It certainly is," I agreed. "I heard the last people who lived there were squatters. There used to be a garden in the courtyard, in back. The house is only nine feet wide. A 'doll house,' the guidebook had called it."

"She could just fall out of bed and roll into Chumley's," Tony noted.

Staring at the tiny urban cottage across the street I felt both light-headed and incredibly sad. It was like watching a lost world . . . a very beautiful and vital one, but one that was irretrievably lost.

"What if they were lovers?" I asked Tony.

"Lovers? Who?"

"Bruno and Edna."

"Was she that promiscuous? Is there anybody she didn't sleep with?"

" 'Promiscuous' is a male word, Tony. You

know, Edmund Wilson wanted to marry her even after he'd been in bed with her and a fellow writer. No, Tony, she wasn't promiscuous. She was trying to be free, even for one moment. She was trying to break out. Don't you understand?"

He started to say something but I shut him up with a savage movement of my hand. "No, Tony! I think I got it wrong. They weren't lovers. But Bruno loved her, like many men loved her. And he couldn't have her. Who knows why? Perhaps he was too crazy or too ugly for her. Perhaps she despised his poems. Yes, that seems right, doesn't it, Tony? That Bruno wrote his heart out but never got anywhere with his poetry. He watched her in the bars with John Reed and Eugene O'Neill. He hung around just to catch a glimpse of her, followed her on the street. She broke his heart. She probably didn't know him from Adam, but she broke his heart. She was a promise . . . a dream . . . his muse in every sense of the word."

"Hmm. I can identify with that. But so what?"

"I think I will be able to show you 'so what' shortly. But first we all have a lot of work to do."

"Now?"

"No, not now, Tony. In the morning. We're going home to make love now."

We held hands as we walked. Even if Basillio didn't believe in it, it felt like 1924 to me.

13

Alison arrived early the next morning, just past eight. She was carrying with her a large bag stamped with the name of a sweet little place up Hudson Street that did catering in the neighborhood and served sandwiches and such to the lunchtime hordes. In the bag were half a dozen fresh muffins, Alison told us: one for herself, one for me, and four for Tony, whom we all knew to be just a little greedy, she said, chuckling. It was no more than a gentle skirmish in their ongoing war, which I knew had something to do with me, and which was really unbelievably childish. Anyway, we had no time for that now.

I made the coffee. Alison was not happy with the brew. She was too well-mannered to make a direct complaint, but her polite little sips and her tight little lips told of her profound distaste. Too long in France, I suppose.

I was just about to outline my operatives' new assignments to them when the phone rang. It was Libby Trask. She was inviting me to a memorial service for Dr. Leon, to take place the following morning in the vestry of the Village Temple, near Washington Square. I thanked her very much for thinking of me but said I wouldn't be able to attend.

After that phone call we all got down to business. "You were both brilliant in your last assignments, troops," I joked, "but now you have a *really* difficult project—each of you. I want you, Alison, to compile for me, as quickly as you possibly can, a chronology of Edna Saint Vincent Millay's life. You can excerpt it from any number of books in the library . . . biographies, literary studies . . . other memoirs . . . whatever you find. What I'm looking for are the concrete events in her life. Where she lived, bought her lingerie, who took out her tonsils—items like that."

I turned to Tony: "As for you, I need something that I really don't know how you can acquire. But I need it. Get me a listing of the major crimes committed by the Italian anarchists in New York between, say 1919 and 1930."

"Yeah, that can be done," he said reflectively. "The trouble is, the newspapers aren't reliable. If I remember, many anarchists were deported after 1920. Those who remained went deep underground and when they robbed banks, for example, no longer issued communiqués of what they had done. But there are some studies of the individual groups and their activities. I know I can get information on, for example, Gruppo Gaetano Bresei, which operated in East Harlem and was named after the anarchist who assassinated King Umberto of Italy at the turn of the century."

"I need it quickly," I said.

"Why? What's the rush?"

"The angel of death, Tony."

"Damn, you're getting dramatic."

"When two people die at your doorstep, you tend to."

"Are we getting warm, Aunt Alice?" Alison asked.

"We're practically in the toaster, my sweet."

"How about telling us why you think that?" Tony said.

"I told you most of it—last night, on Bedford Street."

"I mean, put it all together for your staff. I mean, after all, we're the only staff you have." He was twitting me. But he was also serious.

"Everything in its season, Basillio."

"Yeah. But I'm not a pomegranate."

Alison interceded: "Well, when this mess

is finished at least you'll be able to work on your loft."

I laughed and looked around. It was strange. The more people there were in the loft, the emptier it looked. I wondered if that formula applied to felines as well. A kitten would be nice.

After they left I gave Bushy and Pancho some extra treats. As Bushy was consuming his, I said: "You'll never guess where I'm going now." He paused just for a moment, reflected, then continued eating, not willing to hazard a guess.

I dressed as if I were going to paint a house—jeans and ragged shirt and old boots. Then I walked to Bleecker Street and found the Italian bakery, where I glided swiftly past the bored counterman who was piling up ovals of fresh-out-of-the-oven prosciutto breads. In another minute I was standing in the sunshine as it filtered through the wire mesh arching over the Foundation.

Nothing had changed. As though preserved in amber, Simone was in her chair. Claire was doing her chores. The older cats were moving around comfortably in their protected little world—infirmities aside. The kittens scampered from one side of the fence to the other, leaping and rolling, stopping occasionally to nip at Simone's blanket.

Claire Agoste didn't even greet me. She

behaved not only as if I'd been expected but as if I were twenty minutes late. Without even speaking, she put me to work. The old woman just pointed at bowls to be filled, cement to be hosed, weeds to be plucked.

I carried out the chores without complaining. But I kept a constant watch on her, waiting for a moment of repose, when I could speak to her.

There were a lot of questions I had to ask her. Questions about Bruno, of course. But also about the Village Cat People. Had Danny and Martha really been the only ones of that group to help out? That's what Danny said, but I didn't believe him. There was a good chance that Libby and Ann knew of this place . . . that they were somehow tied in.

When all was said and done it was quite obvious that one of the Village Cat People had both looted Martha's apartment and murdered Dr. Leon. But which one, and why? That was the name of the game—if one could characterize all this heartache as a game. There was no doubt that locked in these old women's heads were the secrets that tied Bruno to Millay . . . which tied both of them to Martha and Leon. It was only Claire Agoste who held the key to a secret so important that people would murder for it decades later.

But the morning evaporated and the old woman never once slowed down. She had no time for conversation. I caught my breath every time I saw her stoop or reach high to perform one task or another, but her wiry old frame always bent; it never broke. She dressed wounds and applied balm to burns. She taped miniature splints to kitty limbs. She administered medication and fed milk with eye droppers. She comforted and chastised. It was an astonishing performance. I kept peering over at her, entranced by the sharpness of her figure, by her fierce eyes and the almost skeletal fury to finish each task.

It was almost one o'clock when she hobbled over to Simone in the wheelchair. She disappeared into the bakery and came back a few minutes later with a wicker tray. Claire sat down on a garden chair near Simone and motioned me over, pointing to a crate I was to use as my seat. She poured hot soup from the thermos into three high-sided bowls. I was given a solitary saltine to accompany my portion. I watched while she fed Simone, roughly wiping the paralyzed woman's mouth when some of the hot soup dribbled out. Not until the entire bowl was finished did Claire begin her own lunch. The soup was good—kale—all the richer for being consumed outdoors. It had the staff-of-life quality over which grandmothers of every ethnic group seem to claim exclusive control.

Now was my chance.

"I'd like to talk more about Bruno," I began, pleasantly enough. "Do you remember the words of Bruno's poem—'Madonna at the Bar'?"

"Martha has the poems," she retorted sharply.

"Martha is dead. The poems have been stolen," I told her.

She laughed in the strangest manner. "Martha has those poems," she said. "Martha is putting them on a computer. She is giving me thousands of copies."

"Was Bruno in love with Edna?" I asked.

She stared at me harshly, then gave Simone's chin a gratuitous pass with a paper napkin.

"Do you know that name?" I pressed. "Edna Saint Vincent Millay. Was she the Madonna at the Bar?"

She shrugged her shoulders. "A woman. It was a beautiful woman." Her face softened. She smiled. "But not like you. You are golden haired." She reached across the years and touched me on the temple.

Then she started to walk away to continue her work.

"Claire!" I called out sharply. "Was it Bruno who taught you those words?"

She stared at me.

"You know what I'm talking about," I pushed. "That anarchist slogan you used. No gods. No laws. No masters. Tell me. Was

Bruno an anarchist? Where did you hear those words first?"

Suddenly her entire body began to tremble.

"Police? You police?" she asked fearfully. I realized my mistake then in asking her that question. She was fixed in the 1920s, when federal agents swooped down and deported anyone they thought was a political threat, an anarchist. Thousands were deported without proof or due process—the infamous Palmer raids.

She ran toward Simone, screaming as she moved: "*Polizia! Polizia!*"

The man from the bakery appeared out of nowhere. He was glaring at me threateningly.

"She has it all wrong," I pleaded with him. "She's confused. I'm not police. I'm a friend. Believe me, a good friend."

"Get out of here now! Right now, lady. Or there'll be trouble. Bad trouble."

It was too late. Claire Agoste was gone. I didn't even have a chance to glance back at Simone. The baker hustled me out of the yard, through the hallway and the bakery, and onto the bustling sidewalk.

I had a terrible headache. It was hard to walk. When I finally got back to my place I flopped down onto the mattress and Bushy curled up next to me in sympathy.

The afternoon turned dark and blustery. I sat listening to the windows rattling. I couldn't sleep or read. I couldn't do anything. Poor Claire Agoste, I thought. I liked and admired that indomitable old woman. The last thing I wanted to do was cause her any pain. And I had ended up terrifying her.

It was an ebullient Alison who broke up the gloom. She arrived back at the loft just before five, carrying her Millay chronology like a banner. She had written it in Magic Marker on the back of a large manila envelope, and she had compiled it from a great number of sources.

It started with Millay's birth in 1892 in Rockland, Maine.

Alison hovered over my shoulder as I read the list. Much of it was known to me—the publication of her poem *Renascence* in 1912, which brought her fame. Her brief stay in Barnard. Her years at Vassar. Her golden years in Greenwich Village. Her work at the Provincetown Players. Her friendship with John Reed and Arthur Davison Ficke. Her love affairs with Floyd Dell and Edmund Wilson and Frank Crowinshield and so many others.

Then Tony came in. I raised my hand in greeting but he saw that I was busy and just sat down across from me at the table.

My eyes went back to the chronological listing. "Good work, good work, Alison." She fairly purred, then moved away from my side and sat down on one of the folding chairs. Now all three of us were at the table.

I ran a finger down the listing some more. I stopped at 1923, when she married Eugene Boissevain.

It was the next entry that gave me a jolt. It stated that Millay and her new husband moved into 75½ Bedford Street in 1924.

"See this?" I turned the chronology around so my two associates could read it. Of course Alison was familiar with it—she had compiled the facts.

"She got married. So what?" Tony offered.

"Well, it seems to confirm my theory of unrequited love. Bruno has been watching her. Longing for her. There is no chance at all now. She is a married woman. She seems to love her husband. Bruno sees them walking across the street to Chumley's together. He watches her holding hands with her beloved at the bar. Poor Bruno . . . his heart is broken . . . he writes the poem 'Madonna at the Bar.'"

"I agree it probably happened that way. But where is all this unrequited love stuff going?"

"Who knows, Tony? Just hang on."

I continued with the chronology.

In 1925 Edna and her husband left the Village and moved upstate—to Austerlitz, New York.

Poor Bruno, I thought. Now even his most remote hopes are dashed. Poor little anarchist.

Then I reached 1927. My expulsive "Oh

my God!" sent Bushy flying in a Pancho-like move up to the top of the refrigerator.

"Look here!" I went on. "I think this is it."

Tony and Alison looked. Tony bit his lip as he read. Alison nodded as she remembered what she had written down. In 1927, a day before the execution of Sacco and Vanzetti, Millay and John Dos Passos were arrested for demonstrating at the Boston State House. Twenty-fours later the execution took place.

"Do you understand the significance of that? Surely you both must. Not only did Bruno have this passionate thing for Millay . . . this love . . . this love . . . but then she puts her freedom on the line for Bruno's compatriots."

"I never knew," Tony commented, "that she had anything to do with the protest movement surrounding Sacco and Vanzetti."

"Well, now you do," I replied. "Wonderful, Alison, you did just wonderful." I stroked her again.

I nodded to Tony. I was ready for his contribution. He slid a small deck of index cards across the table.

"Before you look at these, let me explain. There are about twelve of them. Each one is about a spectacular break-in, usually. I didn't put down the terrorist attacks—the bombings and the shootings. Only where anarchists were suspected of breaking, entering, and robbery. They're incomplete.

Very sketchy. Most of the break-ins were in posh town houses in the Village, Gramercy Park, and Riverdale. Most of the houses were owned by financiers, politicos, or judges. The anarchists hated judges, particularly those who sentenced their comrades to long prison terms—not to mention death."

I started to read the cards. He stopped me again.

"One more thing. The items listed as stolen are even more incomplete. First of all, no complete lists of items appeared in my sources. Second of all, the items were for the most part never recovered because the anarchists didn't rob houses for money. They robbed banks for money. They trashed town houses out of hatred of the rich or vengeance against perceived political oppressors."

I nodded and proceeded.

The first two cards provided nothing—a predictable list of goods taken—silverware, clothes, statuary.

The third card—concerning the robbery of a town house in Washington Square North—listed three stolen paintings, all by Nicolas Poussin.

"Tony, you've done it!" I said and read the entry.

He grabbed the card and looked at it, then handed it to Alison.

We all grinned like the proverbial

Cheshire. We all remembered the art post-cards found in Martha Lorenz's file box, one of which was a reproduction of Poussin's masterpiece, the *Rape of the Sabine Women.*

The fourth and fifth cards yielded nothing.

But with the sixth—suddenly—I saw an entry that rocked me. I must have frightened the two of them, going rigid the way I did. I could see the concern in Basillio's eyes, and I could feel Alison's hand on my arm. "Can we get you something, Aunt Alice? . . . Aunt Alice? . . . Get her some water!" she barked at Tony. I couldn't respond. Dread had taken over my body.

One or the other of them pushed the glass against my lips. I felt as helpless as Simone Ray in her wheelchair. But ultimately I came to my senses. I shook them off.

"Listen to me carefully," I said. "We may all be in great danger, so I will tell you nothing that will implicate you further in this mess."

"What mess?" Alison asked, still alarmed.

I hushed her. "But I need your help. You must come with me tomorrow morning to that memorial service for Dr. Leon. It is there that I am going to bait the grisly trap."

They started to clamor . . . to complain . . . to protest. They accused me of betrayal, of condescension, of fakery. Tony and Alison demanded to know what there was in those index cards that had so deranged me.

"We've earned the right to know," he said bitterly.

He had a point, of course. But I was too afraid to honor that right. So I told them nothing. I convinced them to leave me alone for a few hours. I had work to do. I had to construct the trap. It must be simple. It must be elegant. It must work.

14

It was a short but most difficult walk to the Village Temple the next morning to attend the memorial service for Dr. Leon.

For some reason Alison had begun to resurrect old voodoo-type superstitions she had learned from Senegalese friends in France. As we walked three abreast, it was forbidden to allow any object—tree, pump, lamppost, or another human being—to come between the walkers. "Something awful" could happen if we disobeyed the rule, Alison said. Since Greenwich Village streets are very narrow, the chaos caused was considerable. We were like three drunks trying to avoid a hallucination.

Tony was even more difficult. He was very angry. He kept on muttering how he'd be damned if he'd provide any more help to a woman who didn't confide in him . . . how he was sick and tired of not being appreciated by me . . . how his help so far in this case had been crucial.

Finally, a block before we reached the temple, I said to him sweetly: "Calm down, Tony. You have it all wrong. It's just that I'm unsure. We're all on treacherous ground. Let's just see how it all unfolds. Bear with me, please."

It was the wrong thing to say to him. He stopped in his tracks and began to shout: "*Unsure? Treacherous?* Do you know how pretentious you're beginning to sound, Swede? Maybe you're beginning to believe your press clippings. Is that it? Cat-sitting actress working all alone constructs brilliant traps to bring murderers to justice."

Then, unbelievably, right there on the pavement, to punctuate his anger and derision, he began to recite those lines from *Hamlet.*

> "I'll have these players
> Play something like the murder of my
>   father
> Before mine uncle; I'll observe his looks;
> I'll test him to the quick: If he but
>   blench
> I know my course. . . .
>   the play's the thing
> Wherein I'll catch the conscience of the
>   King."

Then he realized what a fool he was making of himself; even the jaded Villagers were stopping to watch this lunatic bad performance. He was quiet for the remaining block.

The moment we reached the steps of the renovated brownstone that housed the Village Temple I heard my name being called.

It was Detective Crowley, standing near the curb, rocking on his heels. I told Tony and Alison I would meet them in the vestry, and walked over to the police officer. He had a kind of accusatory glint in his eye, and he got right to the point.

"We have found out that Leon and Martha Lorenz were lovers," he said.

"I surmised as much," I said.

"Oh, did you? Well, then, why didn't you tell me when I interviewed you?"

"At that point, if I recall, I hadn't surmised it. Besides, what did it matter to you? The Martha Lorenz case had been cleared."

"It's not up to you, Miss Nestleton, to tell me what information I need and what information I don't need."

"Sorry."

"By the way, I spoke to the detective on the Lorenz case. It's all sewed up."

"So I heard."

"He told me you are a friend of Lieutenant Rothwax in RETRO."

"I used to work with him," I replied. I wondered uneasily whether Rothwax had told Vargas about my rather foolish infatuation with one of RETRO's detectives . . . a very young and very handsome Eurasian. If Rothwax told Vargas, then Vargas told Crowley.

"I also understand, Miss Nestleton, that you fancy yourself as a criminal investigator."

"Just a concerned citizen, Detective."

"Well, as just a concerned citizen, is there anything else you know about Dr. Leon that you haven't told me?"

"Not really."

He flicked out a card and handed it to me. "Call me the minute you think of anything," he ordered. He started to saunter away.

"Aren't you going to the memorial service, Detective Crowley?"

He stopped, smiled, and said, "I'll see everyone who goes in and out. That's enough for one day."

I walked inside the building, down the stairs, and into the vestry. It was just a large wood-paneled room with a raised podium and six rows of chairs.

Along one wall was a table with a white cloth on which were coffee urns, platters of bread and cheese and bowls of cut fruit.

I sat down in the third row next to Tony and Alison. All the Village Cat People were in attendance. Ann and Libby flanked a jumpy-looking Danny Celestino. Peg Oates was there, too, as well as ten or twelve people I didn't know. They must have been a mixture of personal friends and former clients.

A woman with drawn skin walked up to the podium. She identified herself as Dr. Leon's sister. She said that many years ago her brother had left her instructions that when he died he wanted to be cremated and his ashes strewn over their parents' graves—with no religious ceremony whatever.

She had complied with that request, but she thought it proper to bring together a few people who loved him. Not to mourn his death but to celebrate his life.

Then she looked up, expecting looks and murmurs of affirmation, I suppose. But the group was silent. Not because what she had said was unappreciated but because the Age of AIDS had made most of us in the audience almost numb to speech concerning the dead. We had just gone to too many funerals, heard too many orations.

But then Leon's sister did a charming and totally unexpected thing. She noted that her brother was a music lover and above all he loved the blues. Then she picked up a portable cassette player, switched it on, and we all had the joy of listening to Big Mama Thornton's sad, lewd, strangely cosmic rendition of the original "Hound Dog." It was the proper kind of song for a veterinarian to love. There was delighted laughter from the ranks.

After Dr. Leon's sister took her seat again, the young rabbi walked to the podium. He asked us all to bow our heads. We did. He recited a blessing in English. Then he asked us to stand while he recited the prayer for the dead in Hebrew.

The mood had lightened considerably by the time we adjourned to the table with the drinks and food.

I hung on the outside of the circle, waiting for my chance to bait the trap. I was nervous. The palms of my hands were moist and I felt a funny throbbing in my throat.

It was one of the people I didn't know who provided me with the stage cue.

She was speaking to Leon's sister: "Your brother had become a Village landmark. The neighborhood doesn't seem the same without him."

Enter Alice Nestleton, stage left. She is a little brash.

I opened with, "Tragically, there's another beloved Village landmark that's about to be lost."

Everyone stopped chatting and stared at me.

Then Ann Walters said, "I thought you just moved to the Village. Maybe, Miss Nestleton, you ought to wait until you know what the landmarks are." It was an icily sardonic remark and I wasn't expecting it; especially from her.

But I recovered quickly. I always do, on stage.

"That beautiful little house on Bedford Street is about to be bulldozed," I announced, taking a handful of mixed nuts.

"Which house?" inquired the elderly man standing next to Ann.

"That tiny one on Bedford Street."

"You mean Edna Saint Vincent Millay's old frame house?" Dr. Leon's sister asked, horrified.

"Right," I said. "Number $75\frac{1}{2}$ Bedford Street."

"That's incredible," the rabbi said, putting his coffee cup down on the table, "but are you sure you have your facts right? I thought that whole street had become an historic area and nothing could be razed or even renovated."

I was prepared for such an objection. I lied with skill: "It is an historic area. But there is one loophole. If a dwelling is so old and so crumbling as to endanger lives and adjoining property, it can be razed. The new owner obtained engineering surveys to that effect."

There was all kinds of murmuring in the vestry.

Then I activated the trap.

"What makes it even sadder is that two close friends of Dr. Leon are going to be hurt by this atrocious razing."

Now all ears were perked up. I counted

five for maximum drama; then baited the hook.

"Dr. Leon gave freely of his time and talent to two old women on Bleecker Street who run a makeshift shelter for cats. This shelter is called the Foundation. It was started, believe it or not, in the 1920s, with money donated by a legendary old Village poet named Bruno. This Bruno was in love with Edna Saint Vincent Millay and when he died his ashes were given to her. She buried them in her courtyard at 75½ Bedford. The same courtyard that is going to be razed. And for those two lovely old women, that courtyard is a sacred burial site. You can imagine how they feel."

I stopped talking and let the story sink in. People began muttering about the sadness of it all.

Suddenly Libby Trask blurted out, angrily, accusingly: "Are you going to pass the collection basket now?"

I didn't know what to say. So I said nothing. The trap had been set. Everything in my story, of course, was either a lie, a fabrication, a fantasy, or a possibility. I had no proof that Dr. Leon even knew of the Foundation. If he was having an affair with Martha, he must have. And his fantasy about a high-tech feline hospice seemed to point to the possibility that he was inspired by the Foundation. As for where Bruno's ashes were buried, even Claire Agoste didn't know.

I didn't have any coffee or cake after my speech. I walked out quickly after saying goodbye to a startled Alison, who had to meet her true love uptown. She started to ask me about my little speech, but I cut her off gently.

"Tomorrow," I said to her.

Tony followed me out onto the street. We started to walk. He was silent. Suddenly, about a block from the Village Temple, he grabbed me and kissed me.

"You were brilliant, Swede!"

"Thank you."

"Someone's going to dig up that courtyard as fast as he or she can get a shovel. Right?"

"Right, Tony."

"But they won't be digging for old Bruno's ashes, will they?"

"No they won't, Tony."

He grinned from ear to ear. "They'll be digging for anarchist treasure . . . it'll be Treasure Island on Bedford Street."

"You've got it, Tony."

He kissed me again. I pushed him away.

"We have a few stops to make," I said.

Tony and I walked to Bedford Street, turned the corner at Commerce, walked a few feet, and stopped in front of an old iron fence.

"What's this?" he asked.

"Look inside," I ordered.

As he peered through the fence I explained. "You're looking at the communal courtyard for three houses on Bedford Street. This fence is always kept locked. The people in their houses just step out of their back doors into it. Like Edna Saint Vincent Millay did."

I looked through the fence after he had stepped aside. The yard was run down; a small vegetable plot; old flagstones crumbling; a pathetic bird feeder. Not much of anything.

I stepped back and looked at the top of the ancient fence. No barbed wire. Easy to scale. The lock was irrelevant.

"One more stop, Tony," I said. We walked west along the curving Commerce Street until we reached the restaurant on the corner.

"That's the old Blue Mill Tavern, isn't it?" Tony asked. "I remember the actors I knew who studied with Berghoff and Hagen either drank at the Cookie Bar, farther up Hudson Street, or they drank here at the Blue Mill."

"Yes. Except it isn't called that anymore. It's now called Heartland. Something to do with the new owner being from the Midwest."

It was a few minutes after eleven-thirty. Heartland, just opening for lunch, was empty. The lady bartender was still doing her opening chores—slicing lemons and limes.

I ordered, rather flamboyantly, a bottle of Bass Ale and two glasses.

"Let's sit at the small booth near the window," I suggested.

Once seated, Tony poured the ale. We clinked glasses. "To Bruno," he said and then added portentously, "awaiting the hour of vengeance."

I drank my ale lustily. It was delicious. I put the glass down and wiped my mouth with a napkin.

"Look out your window, Tony," I suggested.

He did, and said, "Nice view."

Yes, it was nice. Beautiful in fact. There was a perfect, unimpeded view of that old iron fence around Edna's backyard.

"One more thing, Tony. We need a camera with some fast film."

"No problem."

I leaned back in the booth, suddenly exhausted.

Then with closed eyes I said to Tony: "Our vigil will start around an hour before midnight. Right here, in this bar, at this booth."

"Do you mind if I go home for a few hours now and do the laundry?" he asked.

I was too spent to laugh.

15

By ten forty-five in the evening, we were comfortably ensconced in our observation booth in Heartland. Tony was wearing a slick black turtleneck with a red heart over the breast. Around his neck was the camera. He looked like an aging paparazzi.

Actually we had entered the bar an hour earlier, but our booth had been taken. So we stayed by the bar, keeping watch, ready to swoop when it was vacated. And swoop we did.

"I think this should be your last brandy," I said.

"Right, boss."

On the table between us was the ale bottle, the brandy glass, and a small dish of organic pretzels, or some such animal. They were loathsome.

"What time do you figure Long John Silver and his pirates will show up?" Tony asked.

"I figure any time between midnight and four. And I figure there will be only one pirate."

"Man or woman?" Tony asked.

"I don't know."

"Fat or skinny?"

"Unresolved."

"Black or white?"

"Undetermined."

"Damn your lying eyes," he said happily, finished his brandy, and ordered another, in spite of my specific request to the contrary.

I stared gloomily out the window. The rainy weather was still with us. It was cool and damp outside. But the gate to the courtyard was clearly visible. Had the trap been baited with enough succulent bait? Time would tell.

"Are we just going to sit here hour after hour without talking?" Tony asked, now in his pouting mood.

"What do you want to talk about, Tony?"

"Eros and death," he said happily.

"Not interested."

"Your grandmother?"

"Too nostalgic."

"Pancho?"

"Maybe."

"Good! Because I think it is quite evident that your cat Pancho needs major psychiatric intervention. He's crazy, Swede."

"End of Pancho conversation," I declared.

"Okay. What about the theater?"

"What about it?"

"We can talk about it."

"Like we used to, Tony? Spare me."

"You're getting to be a very cynical lady, Alice Nestleton, aka Swede."

That ended our attempt at conversation for a while.

But at twelve minutes past midnight we had an ugly little exchange, after he ordered another brandy.

When we calmed down, Tony ordered a grilled chicken sandwich. I wasn't hungry but ordered a small Caesar salad to justify our continued occupation of the booth.

Tony became mellower when the taped music in the bar made the switch from the greatest hits of the Eagles to Duke Ellington medleys. With "Prelude to a Kiss" he reached over and began to stroke my fingertips. "Promise we'll make love like never before when all this is over," he said wistfully.

"Promise you'll knock off the brandy."

"Ah, Alice," he said rather sadly. "You're getting old."

"Yes. I know."

I watched the clock. God, what a long day it had been.

"Stop looking at the clock, Swede. You're making me nervous. I can't digest my food."

"Stop calling me Swede, Tony. I'm getting sick of it."

"Why? You look like a Swede."

"But I'm not Swedish. My people are English-Scotch. With a little Norwegian thrown in. And one of my great-aunts married a Shoshone. Besides, I don't even think Swedish people like being called Swedes."

"You're quibbling, Swede. Look, you can call me anything. I don't mind. After all, I'm Italian on both sides. Although one of my distant cousins married a Greek Jew and Uncle Mario, who went to Argentina, married an Amazon woman, so I've been told."

"If he's like you, Tony, I'm sure she shrunk his head."

He found that very funny. He burst out into one of his alcoholic guffaws, which always sounded a little like W.C. Fields.

Then I saw the figure moving slowly along Commerce Street.

"Quiet!" I shushed him.

We both stared out the window. The figure was walking toward Bedford Street.

"Is it a man or a woman?" Tony whispered.

I couldn't tell.

"He's stopping by the gate!" Tony was providing an utterly unnecessary narration of events. I could observe the same things he saw.

But then the figure moved on.

I sat back. The sweat had broken out on my forehead.

"Guess he was just a stroller," Tony commented.

I was about to, finally, taste the Caesar

salad when I saw that the figure was dou-
bling back—crossing on the far side and
then moving west on Commerce.

"Look, Tony! He's just across from the
gate now."

Indeed! The figure was directly across.

And then, almost casually, elegantly, the
figure walked across the street and climbed
the fence.

"He's in the courtyard!" Basillio almost
shouted. Then he slipped out of the booth
and removed the camera from around his
neck.

"Remember, Tony, don't confront him for
any reason. Just walk past. Get some shots.
Make three or four passes and meet me
around front. Don't forget, whoever that is
could be a killer."

"Relax, Swede," Tony said, patting me on
the head. I wondered how the brandy would
affect him on the street. He walked out of
the bar and down Commerce Street. He appeared steady. He held the camera in one
hand and took the shots through the gate
without sighting—like a war correspondent.

He made one more walk-by than he was
supposed to. I cursed him under my breath
but loved him more for it.

Then Tony started walking back to the
bar. I fumbled twenty dollars out of my
purse, added another ten, and rushed out
to meet him. My heart was going thump
thump thump. So far, everything had gone

exactly as planned, as hoped. It was the excitement of perfection.

And we knew exactly what to do next. We ran to Hudson Street, hailed a cab, and drove to a preselected all-night photo lab on West 44th Street and 11th Avenue, the rim of Hell's Kitchen.

The proprietors of the lab knew Tony well from when he owned a chain of full-service copy shops called Mother Courage.

They greeted Basillio like an old friend. Unfortunately, the accommodations in the stuffy anteroom where they said we might wait were much less welcoming. The only place we could find to sit was a small, hard bench without a back.

"It's the same way it was in the maternity hospital, when I first became a father," Tony noted.

I was too keyed up to speak, as nervous as a cat. My ears twitched at every sound.

This was the payoff. I was counting on those photos to clarify things . . . put them in perspective. My worst fears would either be dispersed or confirmed. The photos would reveal to me who and what I was dealing with. Theories and hunches and clues would all go up in smoke from the white hot reality of these beautiful photographs. White hot reality! Bless it!

"Who invented the camera?" I asked Tony.

"Beethoven," he replied. "And Brahms invented the bicycle. And Brecht aluminum foil."

Well, I had put him through a lot lately. It was past three in the morning. Boys will be boys.

We waited on that bench for ninety-one minutes. Then a man stuck his head in the anteroom and said, simply, "Done."

Tony and I rushed to the main counter area. A large manila envelope and a bill were waiting for us.

Tony shook the photos out of the envelope like they were our share of a jewel heist.

"I am one helluva photographer," he crowed as he lined them up.

"I felt my legs buckle. Yes, he had done a wonderful job. They were crisp, clear, focused.

There were two problems.

First, the minor problem. The intruder wasn't digging for anything. He was merely taking photographs of the courtyard, just as Tony was taking photographs of him. But this could probably be explained: He was being careful, probably doing some preliminary work before starting his dig.

The second problem made me sick to my stomach.

The intruder was a white male about twenty-five years old with long sandy hair.

I had never seen him before in my life. Never!

Tony saw my face. "We didn't hit pay dirt, did we?"

"No."

He put his arm consolingly around my shoulder. "Still, Swede, it was a beautiful trap."

"Yes, it was," I agreed. For a brief moment I wondered whether it just was a case of random coincidence. A stranger strolling by the courtyard decided to hop the fence and take photos. A deranged tourist, perhaps. A drunk professor of American literature who did his thesis on Edna St. Vincent Millay, perhaps. No. That was implausible.

"What do we do now?" Tony asked.

"Call Detective Crowley."

"It's nearly four in the morning."

"So it is, Tony. So it is."

I dug out a quarter, went to the pay phone, and dialed the number of the detective. A machine picked up.

"This is Alice Nestleton. It is four A.M. I have important information on the Leon murder. Please meet me as soon as you get this message. The earlier the better. I will be in one of the rear booths in the Lost Diner, at West and Leroy streets."

I hung up and walked back to the counter. "Bring the photos, Tony."

"I'm very tired," he said.

So there we were in the wee hours of the morning, in the Lost Diner, with a few other lost souls.

The burly trucker eating smothered pork chops and garlic mashed potatoes was not the ordinary client of the diner. No, the usual crowd seemed a lot "hipper"—fashion industry types and self-styled artists and employees from the growing number of publishing companies in nearby office buildings. So the diner's aura of 1950s American grunge was all artifice. The kitchen handled as much goat cheese as it did grease, and there wasn't a Bill Haley and the Comets song within a mile of the vintage red jukebox. Most important, I thought the food was wonderful.

Tony fell fast asleep in the booth, stretched out.

I became ravenous, which often happens to me when I am a great deal confused and a bit frightened.

I ordered poached eggs and bacon and one half a cantaloupe. I asked the waiter for a double basket of their homemade biscuits.

The manila envelope containing the photos rested on the end of the table, secured by a sugar dispenser.

The food was delicious. I finished everything and sat back. There was nothing to think about now, nothing to analyze. The photos of the unknown intruder had to be deciphered first. They were either irrelevant or crucial.

Detective Crowley arrived at twenty minutes past six. He stared morosely at the sleeping Tony. I shook Tony awake. He sat up, dazed. Crowley slid into the seat across from me, next to Tony.

"What have you got for me?" he asked.

"Perhaps the man who murdered Dr. Leon," I replied matter-of-factly.

He looked at me—definitely not his usual pedagogic, almost schoolmarmish demeanor—and might almost have been smiling. Except there was no light whatever in his eyes. Just fatigue. And the unspoken admonition that this had better be good.

I pulled the photos out and arranged them in a row. Tony leaned over. I sat up straight.

Detective Crowley immediately took a deep, sharp breath.

Then he said, "What is going on here? What is he doing in there? Where were these photos taken?"

I could tell that Crowley knew the man. It was written all over his face. Was the young man an undercover cop?

"He scaled a fence on Commerce Street. He's taking pictures of the courtyard behind 75½ Bedford Street," I replied.

"Why?" was his simple question. He didn't wait for an answer. He asked another question. "Do you know who it is?"

"No, but you seem to know him."

"Every cop in the precinct knows him. His street name is Jimmy Sly. A very nasty Christopher Street hustler. He's supposed to

be in a locked-down substance abuse facility out in Riverhead."

"I guess the lock broke," Tony quipped.

Crowley ignored him. "This kid gets rough
on occasion. But murder? Not his style."

There was a long, uncomfortable silence.
Crowley kept shifting in his seat. He was
waiting for more. I had nothing more to give
him. He was waiting for me to connect the
courtyard of 75½ Bedford with the murder
of Dr. Leon. I didn't have time. And Crowley
wouldn't have believed me.

Finally, he said wearily: "I can't pick him
up on your say-so." He paused and stared
at the sugar bowl. "But I can talk to him."

"Now," I said urgently. "With me! Because
I know what's in that courtyard."

Another lie. But this one with such dra-
maturgic passion by a trained actress that
Detective Crowley saw visions of a depart-
mental commendation.

Crowley smiled. "Well, the one good thing
about talking to a creep like Jimmy Sly is
you don't need a warrant to enter and
search his domicile."

Crowley's car pulled up at a crumbling,
forbidding red stone building on Charlton,
just east of Washington Street.

"It used to be a garage and repair shop for
that trucking company, Yale Transport,
until they folded. That was about ten years
ago. I heard all kinds of rumors about it—

that it was going to become a hotel—a big disco—a trade school. Even a drug treatment facility."

Crowley laughed and then continued, "But the only thing it ever became is a roosting place for pigeons, rats, a few derelicts, and Jimmy Sly."

We climbed out of the car and followed Crowley up a wretched, rusted ramp. Two smashed-in doors allowed easy access to the building if one could negotiate the jagged edges.

Crowley paused for a moment before entering. He drew his service revolver and held it by his side, close to the thigh. He flicked on a flashlight he had brought from the car with his free hand because even though it was a bright morning, little light filtered into the building.

We walked slowly along the wall. The floor was encrusted, filled with puddles, littered with crushed cartons and undefined objects. There was a sour, stale odor in the air. We heard rustling and chirping, but no genuine human sounds.

Then Crowley called out in a very loud, slow voice; "Jimmy Sly. This is Detective Crowley. Just relax. Just relax."

There was no answer.

We turned a corner and Crowley's light illuminated Jimmy Sly's "room."

It was a filthy space. A mattress on the floor. Several crates on which lay clothing and canned goods. Three cartons of cigarettes on a makeshift wall shelf. The world of Jimmy Sly. Isolated. Damp. Dirty. So depressing the onlooker just wanted to get on her knees and pray.

"I guess Jimmy's out. You know these high-rent buildings. Tenants eat out all the time. He's probably at breakfast." Crowley seemed to have a weird affection for the hustler in spite of his venom.

Then, using his foot and his hands, he picked up and flipped the mattress over.

"Look!" Tony shouted.

The flashlight beam hovered around an ugly metal object.

"Why are hustlers so stupid?" Crowley asked no one in particular.

He took out a ballpoint pen and bent down, inserted the pen into the trigger guard, and lifted up the handgun.

"A Czech-made .25-caliber semiautomatic," he announced. Then added: "The same kind of weapon that killed Leon."

Tony said with awe: "How does a petty hustler get a weapon like that? And how can he afford one of those high-priced Nikons that he was using in the courtyard?"

"He steals." Crowley chuckled to himself.

I bent over to look at the weapon more closely.

"Get out of my light," Crowley barked.

I backed away instinctively. But then I asked him: "What did you say?"

"I said to get out of my light for a minute . . . while I'm checking out the weapon."

I started to giggle. Then laugh.

Someone else had used those same words recently . . . in a story.

And I remembered who.

And I recalled something else. Something a philosophy teacher had once said about Diogenes the Cynic.

I stood on my toes and did a reasonable facsimile of a pirouette.

"You better keep an eye on your friend," Crowley told Tony as if I was cracking up.

I ran to Crowley's side. It was all I could do not to plant a big kiss on his brow. "There's nothing wrong with me, Detective. I'm just happy. You know why?"

"Because you appear to be right about Jimmy Sly? He may well have been the shooter."

"Oh, of course I'm happy about that. But what makes me even happier is that I can also deliver to you now the person who hired the shooter."

"Are you serious?" Crowley asked.

"Quite serious. Please come along."

At about seven-thirty in the morning we parked in front of Dr. Leon's office.

"I'd like to go in there first, without you, Detective Crowley. Just Tony and me."

He laughed. "At this point in time, lady,

you can do no wrong. I'll sit here as long as you want."

A haulage truck was in front of our parked car. Two men brought a sofa out of Dr. Leon's office . . . the sofa that had been in the waiting room . . . and dumped it into the truck. Obviously the office was being made ready for the next tenant.

We walked through the waiting room and into the clinic area. Peg Oates was dumping files. She wore a bandanna tied around her head. She didn't greet us. Not a single word. She just intensified the flinging of the papers into several large garbage bags.

There was no place to sit anymore. And one had to be careful where one stood because all the cabinets were open. I narrowly missed banging my head on an open door at least three times as I maneuvered around the room.

"Can I speak to you for a minute?" I asked finally when it was obvious that no response would be forthcoming.

No answer. No eye contact. Just the rustle of paper and the banging of drawers.

"You ought to speak to me, Peg, because I just came from an old friend of yours—Jimmy Sly."

It was a lie, of course, but it worked. She stopped tying the twist-'um around the neck of an oversized trashbag. She stared at me.

"Yes. He was very talkative, Peg. To the

police. He told them you had ordered and paid for the murder of Dr. Leon."

She screamed at me in response: "How can you believe anything that slimy man says?"

I smiled at her: "So you *do* know him, Peg. You know him quite well. He said you ordered the murder, Peg. He told the police that you paid for it." I gave the rack another turn.

Peg reached out suddenly with one arm and grasped the corner of a cabinet. She was trying to steady herself. The color drained from her face. She had knocked several files onto the floor.

Then she just slid down the wall until she was sitting on the floor like a rag doll. She started to make faces; contorted faces; and I could see that she was trying to speak, but she was overwhelmed by what I had said.

Then she whispered: "It was not supposed to be this way."

"I can't hear you. Please speak louder," I said. For some reason I had no compassion for her. None at all.

"It was not supposed to be murder. I was promised there would be no problems . . . no trouble."

I knelt beside her, very close. "Who promised you, Peg? Was it Felix Drinnan?"

Her mouth moved but no sound came out.

Tony's grip on my shoulder was so harsh that I flinched. "Are you serious? Are you talking about Alison's Felix?" he asked in an astonished whisper, as if we knew three or four other men named Felix Drinnan.

I stood up and moved away from Peg Oates. She seemed to be lapsing into a kind of protopsychotic state.

"Yes, Tony," I said bitterly to him, "I knew it was Felix Drinnan from the time you showed me your lists of anarchist robberies in the 1920s. But I couldn't tell you then. I didn't want Alison to know anything because then Felix would find out. My niece had no reason not to tell him everything. She didn't know what he was. And I didn't want to endanger either of you."

"But how did you know Felix was involved?"

"Because those lists you gave me showed that many collections of rare coins were taken in those anarchist robberies. They were worth a great deal of money then . . . and would have quadrupled in value since then. I'm talking about, for example, a single three-dollar gold piece minted in 1854 that is now worth thirty-five thousand dollars. So I got this chill because Felix is a coin collector . . . a major collector. And suddenly not only did I suspect Felix in the Leon murder but I realized that he had arranged everything so that I would find the anarchist treasure . . . that it had all been a brilliant scam—the loft apartment, his generosity."

"But how did you know Peg Oates was involved?"

"I didn't know until an hour or so ago, when Crowley yelled at me to get out of his light. The first time I spoke to Peg Oates she told me a story about the philosopher Diogenes and Alexander the Great, which ended with that exact same line. But I forgot all about it until Crowley reminded me. Then I remembered something else. Years ago I took a course in Greek philosophy. And the professor told us about Diogenes. How he called upon the Athenians to 'debase the currency.' Everyone thought he meant that in a symbolic sense. But, in fact, Diogenes was a convicted counterfeiter in Sinope and had been exiled from there for his crimes. For that reason, the professor said, Diogenes had always been the favorite philosopher of numismatists. So I put two and two together. It was too much of a coincidence. Yes, Peg Oates worked for Dr. Leon . . . but she probably worked at one time for Felix . . . maybe as a coin scout."

"What the hell is a coin scout?" Tony asked.

"A free-lancer who checks out leads on rare coins."

I turned to Peg Oates to get confirmation but she was still in some kind of shock. She would not respond.

"You still haven't told me why Felix would have Leon murdered."

"Get Detective Crowley here, Tony. I'm too tired to tell it twice."

He walked out and came back two minutes later with Crowley in tow. "This woman wants to tell you about Jimmy Sly," I said, "but first I want to tell you and Tony a very sad story."

Crowley stared at the distraught woman. But he said nothing at all.

I turned a box over, buttressed it with files, and sat down. I tried to squash my excitement. I tried to beat back my weariness. I ended up talking like a pedagogue.

"It begins with Martha Lorenz. She has, like many young women, a passion for Edna Saint Vincent Millay, and the bohemian Greenwich Village she personified. Martha collects items of that period. A harmless hobby. One day, however, she and a fellow worker get involved with an animal shelter run by two very old women. While helping them out, Martha learns that the original benefactor of the shelter was a poet named Bruno. And she finds out that he knew and loved Millay. She also finds out that not only was Bruno a poet but an anarchist who belonged to one of the most feared and successful anarchist groups of the period.

"She becomes obsessed with the idea that a fortune might be hidden somewhere, buried somewhere. And well it might be. She confides in her lover, Dr. Leon. He, too, becomes bitten by the gold bug. But for a different reason. He has this fantastical idea to build an enormous animal hospice up north and staff it with dozens of specially designed animal EMS mobiles.

"Then tragedy strikes. Martha is murdered by an addict in a botched robbery. Leon is ravaged. But not enough to drown out the fantasy. He wants to make sure he has access to all her records, so he loots his dead lover's apartment. And, he confides in his trusty assistant, Peg Oates. She, in turn, mentions it to Felix Drinnan, her old friend. She couldn't know that Felix would become obsessed with the idea of several million dollars in rare coins existing somewhere in Greenwich Village, ready to be dug up. But obsessed he did become. He hired Jimmy Sly to murder Leon, to get him out of the way and get all the documents originally collected by Martha. Felix was demonic. He had Jimmy Sly murder Dr. Leon on my doorstep so that I would renew my investigation and find the treasure ultimately. He could be sure of the latest details because my niece would gladly tell him.

"But he, too, fell for the trap that the treasure was buried along with Bruno's ashes in the courtyard of 75½ Bedford Street. So he sent his assassin. Jimmy Sly. To photograph the terrain. After all, Felix is not your ordinary killer. Is he?"

"Poor Alison," Tony muttered.

Detective Crowley was looking at me

strangely. Then he said: "I'm confused. Just answer this question. Is there an anarchist treasure buried in that yard?"

"I have no idea," I replied.

"Do those old women who run the animal shelter know?"

"One is paralyzed. The other is quite dotty."

"One more question and then I'll deal with Miss Oates who, I assume, will validate all you have said. Who *was* this Edna Saint Vincent Millay?"

"A poet. A woman of valor."

Crowley opened his coat, expansively. He took a step toward Peg Oates who was watching him like a trapped animal. He looked around the room, located a swivel chair with cartons on it, knocked the cartons off and pulled it over to where she was crouching—shaken, pale, trembling.

"Please sit down," he said. She did. In a very gentle voice he spoke to her.

"You may be quite innocent. Or you damn well may be in a great deal of trouble. Either way, just tell the truth. It is the easiest way. Relax. Tell the truth. There is nothing to be afraid of."

Peg Oates stared at him, wide-eyed. Then at me. Then back at him. She was breathing heavily.

"She's a fool," she finally said.

"Who's a fool?" Detective Crowley asked.

"She! She! She's a fool!" Peg Oates screaming, standing and pointing at me.

"Please, relax. Sit down. Relax."

Peg Oates was guided back down gently into her chair.

"Why is she a fool?" Crowley asked, now keeping one of his hands on the back of the chair.

"Yes. I used to work for Felix Drinnan. Years ago. Yes, the money paid to Jimmy Sly was from Felix. But he didn't know what it was for. I borrowed it from him. I told him I needed the money for a down payment on a co-op in Chelsea."

"Did you give the money to Jimmy Sly?" Crowley asked.

"No! No!" She screamed. "I told you. I had no idea what was being planned. I gave the money to Bruno's wife. She said it was to bring an old man, one of Bruno's anarchist friends, over from Italy. A friend who would be able to find what had vanished. Money. Jewels. Paintings. Rare coins."

There was silence. I was stunned.

Had I heard correctly? *Bruno's wife?* The crazed anarchist poet had a wife?

I looked at Tony. He shrugged, more mystified than I was. I didn't feel good. I had the sense that my whole elegant solution was in the process of crumbling.

"If Bruno had a wife, she would be close to ninety by now if she was still alive," I noted, a bit sarcastically for Detective Crowley's benefit.

"At least that," Peggy Oates agreed. The lightbulb went off in my head. Heavy wattage.

"Do you mean that old cat lady Claire Agoste? Are you telling me she was Bruno's wife? Are you telling me she had Dr. Leon murdered?"

"Not her. The other woman. Simone Ray."

"But she's a vegetable! She sits in that wheelchair twenty-four hours a day."

"She's old. And she's sick. But she can walk and talk. The wheelchair is a prop. Her paralysis is a fake. She can feed herself. It's all to make sure she keeps getting the maximum disability. So the cats don't starve."

I was dumbstruck.

"You see," Peg Oates said bitterly to Detective Crowley, "a great deal of what Miss Nestleton said is nonsense, with only a little bit of the truth. Sprinkled about like pepper."

"Then why don't you enlighten us, Miss Oates," Detective Crowley urged.

"Yes, why shouldn't I enlighten you!" she replied sardonically. "It's all over now, isn't it?" She lit a cigarette with a trembling hand.

"I don't know when it started," she began, "but Simone Ray and her friend became friendly with Martha. Simone's married name, by the way, was Fasano . . . Mrs. Bruno Fasano. The old ladies fed Martha stories about an anarchist treasure that Bruno had supposedly hidden from his comrades because the poor deranged man had fallen in love with Edna Saint Vincent Millay. He was going to run away with her and live happily ever after. Martha began her search but unknown to Simone, took her lover Dr. Leon into her confidence. Then Martha died and Leon took all her objects and papers. He told me about it. He was so excited and anticipatory that I believed him."

She paused and stubbed out the cigarette on the floor with her foot, violently.

"So then," she continued, now speaking very quietly, "I decided to do something for myself. I went to Simone Ray. I told her that Dr. Leon was the one who had looted Martha's apartment . . . that he had all the material. I told her that I would become her spy for a price . . . for half of what was recovered. I told her I would keep tabs on the progress of Leon's search. You see, I did not like the much-beloved Dr. Leon. He was an animal lover, not a people lover. And I wanted to get out of this job and this city very badly. I would have been quite happy to betray him and steal the treasure right out from under him. Quite happy!"

She lit another cigarette. She breathed deeply, in and out.

"Then *you* set Dr. Leon up!" I accused.

She smiled grimly. "Yes. I pretended I got

a call from the Village Cat People. I sent Dr. Leon to your loft. But I didn't know he was going to be murdered. And I didn't know Simone Ray had used the money I gave her . . . the money I borrowed from Felix . . . to hire an assassin. Simone told me to fake that call. She told me Jimmy Sly was going to frighten Dr. Leon off the search. She told me he might find it himself and leave us high and dry. I believed her. I was demented. There was something about those old women that made me believe millions of dollars were just waiting to be dug up in Greenwich Village. I never knew that Simone Ray was planning to murder Dr. Leon. Never. Never. Never!"

Detective Crowley pressed her. "But after it happened why didn't you call the police? And why didn't you tell me the truth when I questioned you?"

"Because I was frightened. Because I wanted to get away from the whole business. The murder sobered me up—out of the treasure fantasy."

"You couldn't have sobered up that much," I noted, "because it was you who took the bait when I laid the trap at Dr. Leon's memorial service. You told Simone Ray what I said. And she used Jimmy Sly one more time. Didn't she?"

All Peg Oates did in response was glare at me.

Then Detective Crowley took charge. He

ordered the moving men to cease operations. He called his precinct to send a squad car for Simone and Claire. He asked Tony and me to be on call. Then he left with Peg Oates.

Tony and I were alone.

"Don't be depressed, Swede. It was you who broke the case. It's just that after you broke it, the yolk zigged instead of zagged."

"I'm not depressed, Tony, just pensive."

"The moral of the story is . . . if you're crazy enough to marry an anarchist and survive him by fifty-some odd years—you're crazy enough to believe there's gold in the drains under MacDougal Street."

"And crazy enough," I added, "to murder a man for that nonexistent gold."

Tony put his arm around me. "Amen," he said. Then he whispered in my ear: "But it has to be somewhere, Swede."

I wondered.

16

Seven days later Jimmy Sly and Mrs. Bruno Fasano (aka Simone Ray) were indicted for the murder of Dr. Leon. Peg Oates was indicted on an accessory count.

Jimmy Sly was denied bail. Peg Oates made bail. The old woman was released on her own recognizance and went back to her cats and her wheelchair and her friend—pending trial.

And eight days later I gave a small dinner party in my loft for Tony, Felix, and Alison. The occasion? I had finally purchased a dining-room table and it had been delivered more or less intact: a beautiful old cherry-wood piece, seven feet long and three feet wide.

Dinner was two barbecued chickens . . . rice with spinach . . . corn on the cob—all purchased ready-to-eat from a new-wave "Chicken Delight" emporium that claimed the fowls were basted with organic honey.

Tony arrived first and circled the table critically, after commenting on the beauty of the aluminum-wrapped packages of food on top of the table.

He tapped the table with his knuckles.

"A very pretty piece, Swede."

"Thank you."

"But I thought you were too broke to buy a nineteenth-century French table like this. It had to cost twenty-five hundred dollars."

"No! It's beat up, Tony. Look at the right-hand side."

Tony looked. "You see?" I asked, running my hand over the section of the table where the original wood had been replaced.

"Where'd you get it?"

"At the flea market in the schoolyard on Greenwich and Charles. The man wanted five hundred dollars for it and a fifty-dollar delivery charge. I bargained him down to two hundred and eighty dollars with delivery included."

Tony looked at me with cynical eyes. It was obvious he didn't believe that I had paid so little.

"My next project," I announced, "is chairs. It doesn't seem right sitting at this beautiful table on folding chairs. Does it?"

Tony didn't answer. He just shook his head as if I were out of control in regard to money.

Alison and Felix arrived five minutes later. My niece was positively ebullient. She embraced me. She told me how proud she was of me for helping the police solve the murder of Dr. Leon. And how happy she was to have participated in the investigation, no matter how small her role. She kept on babbling. She was high as a kite.

But Felix was not. And when I saw he couldn't look at me; when I realized he was trying to avoid all contact with me while at the same time trying to be polite—I knew that he knew.

I knew that someone had told him I had accused him . . . to Detective Crowley . . . of masterminding the murder of Dr. Leon.

It had to be Peg Oates who had told him. Felix probably helped her make bail. Yes, it had to be her.

I wanted to crawl into a hole somewhere. The fact that I had accused this very kindly man of a heinous crime . . . a man who had been so good to my niece and me . . . suddenly became almost unbearable. I was filled with shame from the top of my head to the soles of my feet. I was mortified.

The dinner party, for what it was, progressed. We all sat on our folding chairs and ate our goodies. Or rather, Felix and I watched Tony and Alison eat theirs with gusto.

Halfway through the dinner, Felix left the

table to get some water. This was my chance at an apology. I followed him.

"Felix," I said softly, just as he was about to turn on the faucet.

He turned to face me but still kept his eyes delicately averted, as if I had a deformity that he didn't want me to know he acknowledged.

"You know, don't you?" I asked.

He seemed to be struggling with an answer. He obviously didn't want to bring up the whole mess.

Finally, all he did was shrug as if it were nothing and turned back to the faucet.

"Please answer me, Felix. I feel terrible. I want to clear this up."

"There is nothing to feel terrible about," he replied, turning back to me and smiling. For the first time since he had entered my loft he met my gaze directly. He had slipped into his clinical mode.

"I want to apologize. I want to explain, Felix. There were all kinds of facts floating around . . . all kinds of connections. I put them together and the puzzle came out Felix Drinnan. At the time I thought I was being totally objective. But that was fantasy, Felix. The fact was, I just didn't trust you. I didn't like you. So I tarred you with a circumstantial brush. I am very, very sorry. You didn't deserve that kind of treatment."

My confession exhausted me. I didn't know what else to say.

Felix stared at me for a long time and then said: "Well, I figured I was in for some kind of abuse from you, Alice Nestleton, because hot water in this loft is sporadic and I am your landlord."

"Yes," I responded in my best display of acting-class bitterness, "I hate moneygrubbing landlords."

Then we both laughed, embraced, and walked arm in arm back to my new table.

When coffee was served, Tony produced from somewhere a gift-wrapped tube, the kind that one shipped posters or calendars in.

He handed it to a startled Alison across the table, saying: "Happy Birthday!"

"But it's not my birthday," she replied.

Tony guffawed: "So what?"

I was truly startled. Since when did Tony give my niece gifts! There was a very uneasy truce between them that sometimes flared into open enmity.

Gingerly, tentatively, Alison began to strip the gift wrapping from the tube, as if it might explode.

Then she opened the tube, slid the object out, and unrolled it.

"Oh my God!" she yelled. She burst into tears. She stood up and held the poster up for all of us to see.

"It's the most beautiful gift I have ever gotten," she cried.

Yes, Tony had done himself proud. The poster was a photo montage of none other than Maud/Paif, the Abyssinian cat that Alison and her late husband had raised, trained, loved—and lost. The same cat who went on to become an American TV star in perfume commercials. Tony had somehow obtained stills from the videos of Maud/Piaf in her greatest roles and created a collage: cat yawning . . . cat rolling over . . . cat looking affirmative . . . cat looking negative . . . cat in her sinuous, inexplicable beauty.

It was definitely the high point of the dinner party.

After Felix and Alison left I said to Tony: "That was one of the sweetest things I've ever seen you do."

"I wasn't being sweet. I was being practical. Since it was obvious you weren't going to disown your niece, I thought I'd better get friendly with her. I figured it would make me irresistible to you."

"I should have realized you had an ulterior motive."

"You know us theater people . . . corrupt to the core."

When we had finished cleaning up I asked him what he would like to do next.

"Watch the criminal element cavort," he said.

"You mean Pancho?"

"Of course."

So we turned the lights out in the massive loft and watched Pancho sprint hither and thither by the light of the silvery moon.

BE SURE TO CATCH
THE NEXT ALICE NESTLETON
MYSTERY,

*A CAT ON A
WINNING STREAK,*
COMING TO YOU
IN MAY 1995

Chapter 1

It would soon be Valentine's Day. Only six more days. I couldn't wait.

No, that spurious holiday was hardly one of the high points of my year—not usually. I wasn't the little pigtailed blonde all the second-grade farmboys gifted with construction paper hearts and penny candies. Valentine's Day arrived in the middle of February, usually a gray and soul-taxing month in New York City, let alone in Minnesota, where I was born. It has been many more years than I care to recall since a man brought me flowers and called me his valentine. *And*, truth be told, I suffer an actual, visceral disgust at this particular holiday, and have since that long ago February 14 when my ex-husband and I had the row that ended with me falling on the ice in Rockefeller Center and breaking my front tooth.

So what made that upcoming St. Valentine's Day unlike any other? I had a job, that's what.

And I was being driven to it—chauffeured to it—in the backseat of one of those grotesque stretch limousines. Picked up at my own doorstep in Manhattan and driven via the Garden State Parkway . . . to Atlantic City.

I wasn't going to Atlantic City to bet on anything. I'm no gambler. And I wasn't going to catch Wayne Newton or Engelbert Humperdinck either. I was going there to work. I actually had an acting job . . . in Atlantic City.

The marketing manager of a casino-hotel called Monte Carlo, on the famous Boardwalk, had conceived a most unusual Valentine's Day promotion to lure people to his hotel and its gaming tables. The Monte Carlo was putting on a special Valentine's Day extravaganza for lovers who also love the theater. The show was to star a revered and famous actor and an actress whose stature was almost as elevated—in fact, they are husband and wife—in the great love scenes from the world of theater.

Directing the show would be a genuinely talented man—some called him a genius—whose future had once seemed as bright as any star in the heavens—New York, London, Hollywood all at his feet. But his flame had drowned very quickly, at the bottom of the bottle. And so, for years, he made a respectable living and had a fairly respectable career, instead of a stellar one. He directed projects such as the one we were involved in like falling off a log. Until signing on for this particular one, that is. The director dropped dead ten days ago.

There were a few other problems with the production. Chiefly, both leading man and leading lady had backed out when they realized that the casino's first salary offer was also its best and last salary offer. The famous couple could not see their way to accepting wages like that even in the service of a cause such as great theater or continuing education, which was one of their pet charities.

So the Monte Carlo was settling for less in every way. Their first big compromise was me, I suppose. I was offered the leading lady part, and took it, after I-don't-know-who-or-how-many-others turned it down. *Great Lovers Onstage* could just as well have been regarded a brilliant promotional scheme or as the supremely dumb idea I felt it to be. But I don't get paid for telling the people who hire me how to spend their money. Maybe the casino thought it was New Jersey's answer to Monaco. So what? That didn't bother me. If that's what they wanted, I'd play excerpts of every woman in love from Clytemnestra to Nellie Forbush.

The leading man, Gordon Weaver, was not such a big disappointment to the star-conscious people at the casino, I'm sure. Gordon Weaver had risen to stardom in the 1950s as the strong back, long jaw, aw shucks, sweet-talking, song-belting tenor in half the legendary musical comedies on Broadway. He had, as they say, worked with them all He'd even made it into two or three of the movie versions.

As for the new director, one Carlos Weathers, he was about to be famous, the word was. He was on the way up as quickly as the late departed genius had been on the way down. Presumably, there would be a limo waiting for him when his plane landed later in the evening. Mr. Weathers was coming to us fresh from some triumph at a garage theater on the North Side of Chicago.

The monstrosity Gordon Weaver and I were riding in had all kinds of amenities, including a bar, a television set, a small sink, several plush designer towels, and the very latest, very glossiest foreign fashion magazines, to name just a few.

Gordon, after he introduced himself to me in Manhattan, had not said a word since, except for one brief and bitter monologue on how he despised winter. He was a handsome, large man with a full head of wavy brown-gray hair and an archetypal "good" profile, if not a very interesting one.

You would think that two old troupers like us would have a lot to talk about, but it simply wasn't so. Strangers through and through. The only thing he did do during the trip was rattle the ice cubes in his glass—constantly. I wondered why, if he disliked the cold so much, he didn't drink his Jack Daniel's neat.

I leaned back as far as I could in the seat and feigned sleep. Gordon's ice cubes bounced. The car purred. I wished Bushy and Pancho were with me, but I had been warned that no animals whatsoever were allowed in the casino—not dogs or cats or canaries or hamsters or turtles or fish . . . not even, I imagine, a pet bumblebee.

The driver spoke only once the entire trip. He asked if we wished to stop at one of the many roadside fast-food restaurants on the Parkway, to use what he assured us were their spanking-clean rest rooms. I wondered why a vehicle that offered German *Vogue* and Dom Pérignon hadn't managed to provide its own john.

Luckily, neither Gordon nor I was *in extremis*. And so the long, long limo kept moving over the frozen ground.

About an hour outside of Atlantic City I did make a concerted effort to make contact with my leading man.

"Have you ever worked with Carlos Weathers?" I asked.

Gordon flung a couple of fresh ice cubes in his glass and poured another drink. "Mickey Mouse. What does he know?"

I didn't think it was fair to hold Weathers's youth against him. "I hear he's done some very good things in Chicago," I said pleasantly.

Gordon finished his drink and set the empty glass down heavily, as if he were through drinking for the rest of his life. Then he turned and pinned me to the seat with his eyes.

"How long are you in the business?" he asked me. It was an innocuous enough question, but it sounded almost obscene on his lips.

"Nowhere near as long as you," I said.

"Yeah, well . . . you ought to learn how to drink, Cinderella. Before it's all over you'll be doing a lot worse crap than this. I know, see."

I do see, I thought. Gordon Weaver was reminding me that I was not in his league. Just shut up and drink, honey, he was saying. Don't try to match stories with a pro like Gordon Weaver, who's been everywhere and seen everything and could blow his nose on the pathetic salary we'll be getting for this job—seven days' work at a few hundred dollars over scale. Although perhaps these days Mr. Weaver might be using handkerchiefs like the rest of us. He had to have come down a little in the world, otherwise, what was he doing here with me?

So I didn't speak again on the trip. Neither did Gordon and neither did the driver.

Just after six in the evening the vehicle

pulled up in front of the baroque Monte Carlo Casino, at the extreme north end of the Atlantic City boardwalk. It was cold and dark. A fierce wind was coming off the ocean. I could smell the salt water, but I couldn't see anything.

A man came running toward our vehicle, introduced himself as the marketing manager who had arranged the entire thing, Art Agee, and whisked Gordon and me into the hotel.

"Your rooms will be ready in a few minutes. You'll be in our best accommodations, the Winner's Circle, usually reserved for high rollers. Only we don't have very many of those right now. You're on the top floor." He was a confident, very nattily dressed young man. But I really wasn't listening. I was dazzled by the . . . swank . . . of the Monte Carlo. Swank. Like something out of a 1930s film—where was Claudette Colbert in her clingy gold frock by Adrian? Beneath our feet was a long and winding red and gold carpet. Skyward was row upon row of outsized chandeliers, all the same faux crystal, all dripping kitsch. The hotel lobby was circular, with the hotel proper ringing the outside of the central circle with an atrium. In the center were the gaming pits . . . sunken a bit. From any part of the lobby one could just step down into the casino proper. And from any floor of the inside atrium, where the rooms were, one could gaze down on the gamblers.

Art Agee led us on a whirlwind tour of the casino floor: Through the slot machines and computerized poker setups with their hordes of women—women of all ages, single and in groups, all engulfed in clouds of cigarette smoke and high-pitched chatter—pulling maniacally at the levers as if in a trance. And into the more "refined" areas, where the blackjack players sat in a sea of plush green velvet, intent on the cards that seem to be flying from the dealers' fingers. And on to the roulette wheel. And on past the baccarat table. Mr. Agee walked us through the administrative offices behind the cashiers' cage and introduced us briefly to a man called Tobin Haggar, who turned out to be the owner of the casino. Haggar greeted us on the run, so to speak. He was hurrying off to somewhere, and his feet never stopped moving. Still, he managed to come up with a sop to what he must have assumed were our giant show-biz egos. "You're grrr-eat," he said warmly. "Really, both of you. Just great. I love your work. Really." And with that he was gone.

"Let's see the theater," Gordon Weaver then said testily.

The marketing manager looked wounded. "You know, Mr. Weaver, we have a brand-new state-of-the-art theater. By any criteria, particularly acoustics, it is superior to anything on or off Broadway."

Gordon arched his eyebrows and all but snorted.

"But," Agee added, "I thought you knew the performances wouldn't be in the main theater."

"Where then?" Gordon asked.

"Follow me. I'll show you."

We trailed behind him as he walked along the lobby. He stopped when he reached what looked like a large bulge in the wall. It turned out to be one of those open bar areas. And in the center was the abbreviated bar itself, its low-lying shelves filled with bottles.

Behind this was a tiny bandstand on which a Latin combo was tuning up.

Gordon was incredulous. "*This* is it? This is where you expect me to perform?"

Us, I thought. Where they expect *us* to perform, Mister Broadway. But I refrained from speaking. I felt a little light-headed. I guess I was tired. I guess I was hungry. Those were the reasons, I'm sure, I was so tempted to laugh. In fact, I turned away from the two of them briefly so that Gordon Weaver would not see me struggling with my mouth.

"On that *fecockteh* bandstand is where I'm appearing!?"

"Well, yes," Art Agee said, genuinely surprised at Gordon's anger. "The bar area seats about a hundred and fifty people . . . well a hundred or so . . . when filled up . . . on a good night."

Weaver gave me a fleeting glance of utter disgust. Now, he was seeking solidarity with me. Still I said nothing. Our stage wasn't what I had expected either, but I had performed under a lot less commodious circumstances.

"Shall we see if your rooms are ready now?" Agee asked.

We trouped over to the elevator bank. And the moment we stepped into one, Gordon began to mutter: "I hate these things. I hate elevators. And why the hell do they have to make them out of glass? They think that's classy or something? What if you don't *want* to see yourself rising a hundred stories off the ground, huh?"

"There's nothing at all to worry about, Mr. Weaver," Art Agee assured him. "These are state of the art. And they're constantly being maintained."

I wished Art Agee would stop using those words: state of the art.

Gordon Weaver lashed out: "Maintenance won't help if there's a fire. In the fire in Mexico a few years ago, people got roasted to death in the hotel elevators." It was obvious that my leading man had a great fear of flames. In fact, if I had to guess, I'd say Gordon Weaver was a mass of phobias and unreasoning hatreds.

"Yes," Agee countered without skipping a beat, "but their stairwells were locked. Of course we've never had a fire here at the Monte Carlo. But just in case—use the stairs. The doors open easily on each floor, in and out, and they are guaranteed fireproof."

That crisis settled, Art Agee led us to our respective suites.

He had not lied about the accommodations. I'd never stayed in posher quarters. If there was a bed size beyond king, mine was it. All covered in damask and satin. The bathroom was opulent beyond belief—my own whirlpool and fine English soaps and mysterious-scented unguents and enormous fluffy bathsheets and robes and theatrical makeup mirrors and boar's hair brushes and herbal teabags; there was even cable TV and speakers from the stereo system in the main room. I took a look out of my bedroom window. The ocean was there, I could hear and feel it, but it was too dark to see anything but shadows. I noted also the widow's walk on the beachfront window, although it was a fake one with no bottom on which to walk.

At last, Art Agee left me. I undressed quickly and lay down on the bed, then got up to open the window, since they were overdoing the heat a bit. No sooner had I closed my eyes than the phone rang.

It was Gordon Weaver. Did I want to have

dinner with him? I did *not.* I'd pegged Gordon for one of those men who feel as if a limb is missing if they don't have a female on their arm at dinner. I thought, with newfound empathy, of the red-haired actress who'd been, I believe, the second Mrs. Gordon Weaver, who now ran a well thought of, if stodgy little restaurant on the Upper East Side of Manhattan, and who drank a bit, I'd heard.

The phone rang again. This time Art Agee was inviting me to supper. Again I declined, showing minimal manners. I really was tired. The truth was, it was too early to sleep. I ordered a ham sandwich from room service, changed into my night things, and picked up the hotel newsletter from the bedstand. I read all about a certain lady from Virginia who had just won a million dollars playing the slot machines.

At nine-thirty I called my niece, Alison. The cats were fine, she said. Then I phoned Tony Basillio. He wasn't in.

By ten o'clock I was flicking the lights off, and in a matter of minutes was fast asleep.

Four hours later I sat up abruptly, my body bathed in a cold sweat. I swung my legs over the side of the bed, in panic. Where was I? What was happening to me?

Then I realized it had just been a bad dream. I knew where I was.

An evil man had been chasing my two cats, Bushy and Pancho, in a rose-colored tunnel. And they were crying out for my help . . . terrible, pathetic mews.

I gathered my wits. First I had to have a glass of water. And then I had to adjust the thermostat in the room. It was broiling! I might even have mistakenly turned the heat up instead of lowering it earlier.

I got out of bed and walked a little raggedly toward the bathroom.

I heard something!

I stopped walking and held my breath.

There it was again! I *heard* something. I heard a cat mewing!

What was happening? Was I going crazy? The dream was over, wasn't it? I rushed to look under the bed. No. In the closet. No. In the bathroom. No.

Meanwhile the mewing was becoming louder and more pathetic and desperate.

Then I realized it was coming from outside the window I had opened earlier. But how could that be? We were sixteen stories up.

I approached the window slowly. I could see nothing outside. But the sound was definitely coming from out there. Then I quickened my pace and pushed the window open all the way.

A cat jumped into my room. A beautiful, trim, perfectly formed little short hair with fur like spun white gold.

She looked at me and then at her new surroundings. Then matter-of-factly walked to the bed, hopped up, and stretched her little frame out on top of my sheets. The tip of her tail was black and there was a sweet cap of black on her head, between her delicate little ears.

"Who are you?" I asked. "Jean Harlow?"

She paid no attention to me. I went and stuck my head out the window. Where had the cat come from? How was it possible? Was she a stray from the beach who lived under the boardwalk? But how could she climb sixteen floors?

Then I saw the drainpipe that came from the roof and bypassed by a few inches all the fake widow's walks.

I realized there were two possibilities: The cat had either come from the roof and climbed down one story, or had come from the room beneath me and climbed up.

I turned and stared at Harlow. "Well, which is it, girlie? Where'd you come from?"

She yawned expansively and flicked her tail. A very cool feline indeed.

This cat couldn't possibly be a stray. She was much too clean and well groomed. She had to have come from the room beneath. But no pets were allowed in the hotel, Art Agee had told me. He'd been adamant about it, in fact. I thought for a moment. There was no choice. I had to go and find out.

I threw on a bathrobe, told Harlow to stay put, and took the elevator down to the room directly beneath mine. I was so confused and excited that I didn't even realize the inappropriateness of knocking on someone's hotel door at two in the morning.

I needn't have worried, though. The woman who answered did not seem the least bit put out by the intrusion. She was obviously wide awake and altogether friendly.

"What can I do for you?" she asked perkily. She was smiling, standing there in a pair of very expensive silk pajamas I knew the hotel had not provided. A shortish woman in her forties. Around her neck was a woolen muffler and on her feet were big puffy ski boots.

I didn't understand.

I didn't understand the queer way she was dressed. And I didn't understand why the front of her pajamas was stained with blood. Quite a lot of it.

I stepped back instinctively.

"Please. Come in," she said, and moved aside to let me enter.

I wasn't about to do that. But I did look in past her.

On the floor of the room, about ten feet from the door, was another woman. She was naked and there was a lot more blood on her slashed body. It seemed a very safe bet she was dead.

ENTER THE
MYSTERIOUS WORLD OF
ALICE NESTLETON IN
HER LYDIA ADAMSON
SERIES . . . BY READING
THESE OTHER PURR-FECT
CAT CAPERS FROM SIGNET

A CAT IN THE MANGER

Alice Nestleton, an off-off Broadway actress-turned-amateur sleuth, is crazy about cats, particularly her Maine coon, Bushy, and alleycat, Pancho. Alice plans to enjoy a merry little Christmas peacefully cat-sitting at a gorgeous Long Island estate where she expects to be greeted by eight howling Himalayans. Instead, she stumbles across a grisly corpse. Alice has unwittingly become part of a deadly game of high-stakes horse racing, sinister seduction, and missing money. Alice knows she'll have to count on her catlike instincts and (she hopes!) nine lives to solve the murder mystery.

A CAT OF A DIFFERENT COLOR

Alice Nestleton returns home one evening after teaching her acting class at the New School to find a lovestruck student bearing a curious gift—a beautiful white Abyssinian-like cat. The next day, the student is murdered in a Manhattan bar and the rare cat is cat-napped! Alice's feline curiosity prompts her to investigate. As the clues unfold, Alice is led into an underworld of smuggling, blackmail, and murder. Alice sets one of her famous traps to uncover a criminal operation that stretches from downtown Manhattan to South America to the center of New York's diamond district. Alice herself becomes the prey in a cat-and-mouse game before she finds the key to the mystery in a group of unusual cats with an exotic history.

A CAT IN WOLF'S CLOTHING

When two retired city workers are found slain in their apartment, the New York City police discover the same clue that has left them baffled in 17 murder cases in the last 15 years—all of the murder victims were cat owners, and a toy was left for each cat at the murder scene. After reaching one too many dead ends, the police decide to consult New York's cagiest crime-solving cat expert, Alice Nestleton. What appears to be the work of one psychotic, cat-loving murderer leads to a tangled web of intrigue as our heroine becomes convinced that the key to the crimes lies in the cats, which mysteriously vanish after the murders. The trail of clues takes Alice from the secretive small towns of the Adirondacks to the eerie caverns beneath Central Park, where she finds that sometimes cat-worship can lead to murder.

A CAT BY ANY OTHER NAME

A hot New York summer has Alice Nestleton taking a hiatus from the stage and joining a coterie of cat-lovers in cultivating a Manhattan herb garden. When one of the cozy group plunges to her death, Alice is stunned and grief-stricken by the apparent suicide of her close friend. But aided by her two cats, she soon smells a rat. And with the help of her own felinelike instincts, Alice unravels the trail of clues and sets a trap that leads her from the Brooklyn Botanical Gardens right to her own backyard. Could the victim's dearest friends have been her own worst enemies?

A CAT IN THE WINGS

Cats, Christmas, and crime converge when Alice Nestleton finds herself on the prowl for the murderer of a once-world-famous ballet dancer. Alice's close friend has been charged with the crime and it is up to Alice to seek the truth. From Manhattan's meanest streets to the elegant salons of wealthy art patrons, Alice is drawn into a dark and dangerous web of deception, until one very special cat brings Alice the clues she needs to track down the murderer of one of the most imaginative men the ballet world has ever known.

A CAT WITH A FIDDLE

Alice Nestleton's latest job requires her to drive a musician's cat up to rural Massachusetts. The actress, hurt by bad reviews of her latest play, looks forward to a long, restful weekend. But though the woods are beautiful and relaxing, Alice must share the artists' colony with a world-famous quartet beset by rivalries. Her peaceful vacation is shattered when the handsome lady-killer of a pianist turns up murdered. Alice may have a tin ear, but she also has a sharp eye for suspects and a nose for clues. Her investigations lead her from the scenic Berkshire mountains to New York City, but it takes the clue of a rare breed of cats for Alice to piece together the puzzle. Alice has a good idea whodunit, but the local police won't listen, so our intrepid cat-lady is soon baiting a dangerous trap for a killer.

A CAT IN A GLASS HOUSE

Alice Nestleton, after years in off-off Broadway, sees stardom on the horizon at last. Her agent has sent her to a chic Tribeca Chinese restaurant to land a movie part with an up-and-coming film producer. Instead, Alice finds herself right in the middle of cats, crime, and mayhem once again. Before she can place her order, she sees a beautiful red tabby mysteriously perched amid the glass decor of the restaurant . . . and three young thugs pulling out weapons to spray the restaurant with bullets. A waitress is killed, and Alice is certain the cat is missing, too. Teamed up with a handsome, Mandarin-speaking cop, Alice is convinced the missing cat and the murder are related, and she sets out to prove it.

A CAT WITH NO REGRETS

Alice Nestleton is on her way to stardom! Seated aboard a private jet en route to Marseilles, with her cats Bushy and Pancho beside her, she eagerly anticipates her first starring role in a feature film. To her further delight, the producer, Dorothy Dodd, has brought her three beautiful Abyssinian cats along. But on arrival in France, tragedy strikes. Before Alice's horrified eyes, the van driven by Dorothy Dodd goes out of control and crashes, killing the producer immediately. As the cast and crew scramble to keep their film project alive, Alice has an additional worry: what will happen to Dorothy's cats? As more corpses turn up to mar the beautiful Provençal countryside, Alice becomes convinced the suspicious deaths and the valuable cats are related. She sets one of her famous traps to solve the mystery.

Lydia Adamson is the pseudonym of a noted mystery writer who lives in New York.